Hide and Seek

katy grant

Hide and Seek

katy grant

PEACHTREE
ATLANTA

Published by
PEACHTREE PUBLISHERS
1700 Chattahoochee Avenue
Atlanta, Georgia 30318-2112
www.peachtree-online.com

Cover design by Maureen Withee
Book design and composition by Melanie McMahon Ives
Manufactured in the United States of America
10 9 8 7 6 5 4 3 2 1
First Edition

Library of Congress Cataloging-in-Publication Data
Grant, Katy.
  Hide and Seek / written by Katy Grant.
    p. cm.
  Summary: In the remote mountains of Arizona where he lives with his
mother, stepfather, and two sisters, fourteen-year-old Chase discovers two
kidnapped boys and gets caught up in a dangerous adventure when he comes
up with a plan to get them to safety.
  ISBN 978-1-56145-542-3 / 1-56145-542-3
  [1. Coming of age--Fiction. 2. Kidnapping--Fiction. 3. Family life--Arizona--
Fiction. 4. Divorce--Fiction. 5. Survival--Fiction. 6. Arizona--Fiction.] I. Title.
  PZ7.G7667757Gr 2010
  [Fic]--dc22
                                    2009040519

For my husband Eric,
with all my love
—K. G.

Chapter 1

It was a perfect afternoon. The sky was a deep, deep blue and there wasn't a cloud anywhere. The sun was warm on the back of my neck and my shoulders—T-shirt weather. A great day for hunting hidden treasure.

I pushed my mountain bike out of the shed and was ready to take off when my little sister came racing down the back steps of the house.

"Hey, Chase! Are you going to the river to look for crawfish? Wait for me, okay? My bike doesn't have a flat anymore."

There was no way I wanted Shea along today. She'd slow me down.

"I'm not going to the river, Shea. I'm going on a really long bike ride. Stay home, alright? Trust me, you'd be bored."

She narrowed her eyes at me and crossed her arms. "That's the lamest excuse I've heard this century. You know I can keep up."

That was true. She's only ten, but she's a tough little kid, and she loves doing outdoor stuff as much as I do. But there was one thing I knew she liked just as much as being outdoors. "Anyway, Rick needs you to help out at the register, remember?"

"Oh, yeah. Because he's doing inventory. Don't you want to help us?" she asked.

"Maybe later. If I get home in time."

Shea still thought it was fun to work in our family's store. For her, it was almost a game, like playing house. When I was her age, I thought it was fun too. Now it's a lot of work.

Shea is just as good at working the register as my older sister Kendra or me. She always sits behind the counter on a stool and counts change and gives all the tourists fishing advice.

Not that there'd be any tourists today. All the tourists had gone home to Phoenix after Labor Day. I knew Rick would be lucky to sell one carton of night crawlers all afternoon.

I swung one leg over my bike. When Dexter saw what I was up to, he raced over, his ears pushed forward and his tail spinning like a windmill.

"What's in your backpack?" Shea asked me as I rolled through the gravel. "It looks heavy."

"A water bottle and some trail mix and stuff." I didn't tell her exactly what stuff because that would give away what I was doing, and then she'd definitely want to come along. Dexter ran ahead of me. He knew if I was on my bike, it was going to be a fun afternoon.

"Why don't you want me to know where you're going?" she asked suspiciously.

"I'm not exactly sure where I'm going. Just out for a ride, alright? Tell Rick I'll be home by six!" I yelled over my shoulder. It was four o'clock, so that gave me two whole hours.

Whew! Finally. Freedom. All summer I'd been cooped up in our store with my family, working the register and stocking shelves. Selling bait, tackle, soft drinks, marshmallows, or anything else tourists need when they're camping.

Hide and Seek

Got any hand sanitizer?
Yes sir, second aisle on the left, top shelf.
Do you guys sell popcorn?
We sure do. Did you want Jiffy Pop or a bag of already-popped?

Besides the store, my family also owns six cabins, and we're booked solid almost every weekend in the summer. The cabins have to be cleaned, the store shelves have to be stocked, the woodpile has to be replenished. There is *always* something to do.

All three of us kids help out. We have to in the summer. My friends can't believe how much work our parents expect us to do. But it's not like we have a choice. If we complain or "have an attitude" about it, my mom and stepfather give us the standard lecture that we've all heard a hundred times about how this is a "family-owned" business, and "since you're a part of this family, you have to do your share."

So I pretty much just keep my mouth shut and get all my chores done as fast as I can. But it's enough to drive a guy crazy. When summer finally ends and the tourists go home, school starts, and then I'm stuck in a classroom all day. Sometimes you just need to get out and breathe.

This was going to be the first geocache I'd ever done completely on my own, so I'd planned everything carefully. Shea was right—my backpack was heavy. It was full of stuff I might need: a stainless steel water bottle, a plastic bowl for Dexter, some trail mix, beef jerky, binoculars, some extra AA batteries, and a Swiss army knife. And then the items to trade for the geocache, and my GPS so I could find the treasure.

Dexter and I headed north on the 373. "Get in the gravel, Dext," I told him. His ears perked up, and he trotted over to the side of the highway and stayed on the shoulder. Pete Dawson passed by in his old Bronco and tooted at us. I waved back. Other than that, there wasn't a car in sight. The only people on the 373 are either driving into Greer or driving out of it, because once you get through town, the highway just ends.

Dexter had a pattern. He'd run ahead of me about twenty feet, then stop, sniff, and squirt. Run, stop, sniff, squirt. He wanted to make sure every animal for miles around knew this was his rock, his tree, his highway. He stopped at one patch of grass and sniffed for so long I passed him on my bike.

"Anyone you know?" I called over my shoulder. He squirted and ran ahead of me.

I pulled off the highway and Dexter stopped, too, waiting a little ahead of me to see if I was coming. I shrugged off my backpack and pulled out my handheld GPS. My fourteenth birthday was last week, and Dad had given it to me as an early birthday present the last time I saw him in August. "In case you ever get lost up there in the boonies," he'd said. He still finds it hard to believe Mom moved us up to the White Mountains after she married Rick. Dad would never leave Phoenix.

He wasn't really worried about me getting lost. He knew I'd been wanting a GPS of my own so I could try geocaching. We did a few together around Phoenix and he thought it was pretty cool. Today was the first chance I'd had to use my new GPS around here. It had taken me a while to figure out all the different features.

I turned it on and waited for it to find the satellites within range. People take GPS systems totally for granted, but there is amazing technology behind them. This little thing in my hand was picking up signals from satellites orbiting the earth, way up there in the sky.

I had found the coordinates of the cache I was looking for

on the Internet and entered the waypoint into the GPS, so now I could see that we were 5.2 miles away from our destination. I switched screens to the navigation page, the one that looks like a compass, and the arrow pointed slightly northwest. Okay. We were going in the right direction.

Five miles out there and five miles back. That would take a good forty-five minutes to an hour at least. Probably even longer, depending on how rough the terrain was and how fast I could go. Plus I'd need time to find the geocache. I might find it in a few minutes, or it could take me half an hour. And there was always a chance I might not even find it today. I'd be lucky to be home by six. But I'd better try to be. After six o'clock, I'd start running out of daylight fast.

I slung my backpack on my shoulders and we took off, still heading north on the 373. I held the GPS in one hand, propping my wrist against the handlebars for balance when I needed to, but I really only needed one hand to steer with. We were coming up to Sheep's Crossing, and I watched the navigation arrow point west.

"Turn!" I yelled to Dexter, and he turned left, like he knew exactly where we were going. Now we were off the highway and onto a winding mountain road. One side dropped off to a sheer hillside covered by thick stands of trees. On the other side, cabins were tucked away behind spruce, firs, and ponderosa pines. Most of the cabins were rentals that were full all summer. A few of them were vacation homes for Phoenix residents, but they all looked empty now. We passed two new cabins under construction.

This stretch of road was nice and shady, and the air felt cooler here among all these tall trees. The road was climbing pretty steeply now, and I had to stand up and pedal to get up enough momentum. I was panting a little, taking in deep breaths of the warm, piney air that the evergreens gave off in the afternoon sun. I was having trouble holding the GPS, so I slipped it into one of the big pockets in my cargo shorts. Anyway, I knew we were going in the right direction. Our geocache was hidden somewhere out on this road—3.9 miles away to be exact.

After a while, we'd gone far enough that there were no more cabins in sight—just a narrow road that kept winding up the mountain. I was really out of breath now and pumping so hard that I could feel the strain in my leg muscles. I hoped I wouldn't have to get off my bike and push if the hills got too steep.

Finally the road leveled off and I could sit back in the seat again. I caught my breath, filling up my aching lungs with cool mountain air. Dexter trotted along, having the time of his life—run, stop, sniff, squirt. He never got tired. He's part German shepherd, part something else. His back has the black saddle like most shepherds, and his legs are tan, but his ears flop down instead of standing up, and his fur is short. But he's smart like a German shepherd, and he's a great tracking dog. He's always on the trail of some interesting smell.

When we came to the top of the hill, the road rose up out of the trees, and now we were in open meadows. All around us was wide-open space as far as the eye could see. Patches of dry, straw-colored grass rippled as a slow wind passed over them. Overhead, the sky was so intensely blue that I felt like I could dive right into it. I took a deep breath. "Hey, Dexter, notice something?" I yelled to him as he ran ahead of me. Now that we'd leveled off, I could pick up speed. "We've got the mountains to ourselves again. No tourists!" I whooped at the top of my lungs.

Hide and Seek

Mom and Rick don't like us to say anything even slightly negative about tourists. Rick always calls them our lifeblood. "We couldn't survive without them," he says. "So smile and tell every one of them to come back soon. And remember—they don't have to come to Greer. They could take their dollars to Christopher Creek or Forest Lakes or Pinetop-Lakeside. But we want them right here in Greer." *Get your rear to Greer!* our postcards say on the little metal stand by the door.

I know we need them. But it's so crowded in the summer. I have to admit that the fall and spring—the "lean months," as Mom and Rick call them—are my favorite times. It's so peaceful up here when there aren't crowds of people around.

I caught up with Dexter at a trailhead with two wooden posts on either side. The hiking trail stretching out in front of us was a dark ribbon cutting through the swaying grass of the open meadow. I stopped to check the GPS. The navigation arrow pointed west, straight ahead in the direction of the trail. We were 2.3 miles away from our geocache. We went across a little footbridge over a dry gulley, and then the hiking trail followed an old railroad bed. The trail was paved with a bunch of rust-colored cinder rocks that crunched under my tires. Even on a mountain bike, the cinders were a little hard to ride on, and I could feel the jarring pressure as my hands gripped the handlebars.

Now all around us were open fields, and we could see for miles and miles. According to the GPS, we were at an elevation of 8,562 feet. Up here, there weren't a lot of trees, but there were little stands of white-trunked aspen clustered together. Their leaves were still pale green, fluttering silver in the breeze. The aspen hadn't started to turn yet, but pretty soon the whole mountain would be covered in yellow, gold, and orange. The only sound we could hear was the low rustle of the wind waving the branches of the trees above our heads.

I was glad to have Dexter to keep me company. I'd thought about having Chris come along today because he's never been geocaching. He's my best friend at school, but he lives about fifteen miles away from me, so we don't get a lot of time to hang out together after school unless one of us plans on going home with the other. But part of me wanted to be alone to do my first geocache with my new GPS. Could I go out on my own and guide myself to my destination, and then get home safe again? It was something I wanted to try.

My uncle first took us geocaching a couple of years ago when he came out to visit us from Nashville. He showed me how to look up geocache locations on a website and put in the waypoint on his GPS. Then he took Shea and me out and we found a few caches around Big Lake.

My older sister Kendra thought it was weird. "You mean people just hide a bunch of junk in some container for strangers to find later? What's the point?"

Uncle Andy raised one eyebrow at her. "What's the point of *Dance Dance Revolution?*" he asked, to tease her, because at the time she was totally addicted to that game.

"It's good exercise," she told him.

"Well, so is this, because you're walking around. Plus you're outside."

Shea and I loved it. "It's like hide-and-seek," she said.

The cool thing is that non-geocachers—muggles—can pass right by a hidden cache without even knowing it's there. It's like a secret club. And there are over 300,000 geocaches hidden all over the globe. Pretty amazing, considering this sport has only been around since 2000. That was when GPS systems got a lot more accurate and people started using them to guide them to different locations. I haven't hidden my own geocache yet, but I'm going to soon. That'll be pretty cool.

"Dexter, want to find some treasure?" I asked, and his ears pushed forward. We stopped and I took out my water bottle and his plastic bowl. I took a swig, then poured some for him. At first he wasn't interested. He was busy sniffing at a patch of dry grass. Then he came over and sniffed the bowl and took a long, sloppy drink, his muzzle dripping beads of water when he held his head up to look around.

My eyes scanned the meadows around us, and then I spotted them. Elk! A whole herd of them. They were a good five hundred feet to the north of us just over the rise of a hill, grazing in the field.

"Wow!" I whispered to Dexter. "There must be thirty of them!" I dug inside my backpack for my binoculars. It doesn't matter that I've lived in the White Mountains of Arizona almost my whole life, and I see wildlife at least once or twice a week. I still think it's exciting.

I watched the elk herd through my binoculars for a while. I wished we could move closer, but I knew if we tried to, they'd see us and move off into the trees. We were far enough away that Dexter didn't really notice them—if we got close enough for him to see them, he'd want to chase them. It was better to keep a safe distance. All the elk still had their reddish brown summer coats, but pretty soon they'd be shedding those for the darker coats of winter. I could see several calves standing near their mothers, but their coats had lost their baby spots.

September and October are rutting season, and whenever I'm outside during this time of year, I can usually hear elk bugling. It's this loud, blaring moo that starts out in a really low pitch and gets higher and stronger as it goes on. It sounds sort of like a really bad bugle player blowing one long, out-of-tune note for a full thirty seconds. The horrible sound of it is enough to make your eardrums cringe, but the elk sure seem to like it. I guess it means love is in the air.

"We better get going," I said, as if Dexter was the one holding us up. I stuffed the binoculars inside my backpack and we took off down the hiking trail, with me bumping along through the cinders on my bike and Dexter trotting ahead of me. Every now and then I'd stop and check the GPS. The navigation arrow still pointed west, pretty much straight ahead, so I knew we'd find the geocache somewhere along this trail.

We were getting closer and closer—.7 miles, then .4, then .3. Pretty soon we were down to a matter of feet. At that point, I got off my bike and left it beside the trail because it was easier now to navigate on foot. I kept my eye on the screen, and with every step I took, the number of feet ticked down like seconds on a watch: 62 feet, 59, 53, 48, 44 feet—and then I was within 23 feet of the geocache. Now I didn't really need the GPS anymore, so I slipped it into my pocket. It had brought me to within a matter of feet of the waypoint I'd marked, but I had to find the hidden cache on my own.

I scouted out the area. This was an awesome place to hide a geocache because the hiking trail had come right up to a little grove of trees and bushes. Very good spot. Lots of potential hiding places.

I started looking in the bushes, pushing back branches and searching underneath for any signs of a hidden treasure. At the base of a bush was a pile of dead leaves and plant matter. The soil around it was loose; someone could easily hide something in there.

Dexter watched me pawing through the underbrush and ran over, his ears pushed forward and his forehead wrinkled.

His face pretty much asked, "See something alive in there?" but I told him no, we were looking for something else. He wandered off to sniff some elk nuggets.

Since I didn't have much luck in the bushes, I walked around the little grove of trees, looking up in the branches for any signs of a container, maybe hidden in the crook of a branch. There were piles of rocks nearby, and I picked through those to see if anything was buried underneath. So far, nothing. But this was the part I love—when you know you're within feet of the geocache and you just have to find where it's hidden.

I walked around the trees, and that's when I saw the fallen log. "That could be it," I said out loud. "Wouldn't that be a perfect hiding spot?" I was halfway to the log when I spotted a couple of objects nearby in the dirt. Seeing those things stopped me right in my tracks.

Uh-oh. This was not a good sign. My heart sank at the sight of the small toys scattered around by the fallen log.

A little green army man was lying on his side in the red dust. Next to him was a die-cast Jeep. I could still see the tracks in the dust where the toy Jeep had been doing dough-nuts. Dexter walked over to them cautiously and gave them a thorough sniff.

"Who is it, Dexter? Does it smell like muggles?"

Dexter walked away and squirted in the grass to let the muggles know he'd been here too. I looked around as if I expected to see the people who'd taken the toys out of the geocache, but of course no one was around. Dexter and I were all alone out here.

I bent down and looked inside the end of the log, but I didn't see anything. I grabbed a stick and poked around inside until I hit something hard. It made a hollow metal sound when I hit it with the stick. I reached inside the log and felt around. Under a pile of leaves I could feel some kind of metal box.

I pulled it out and brushed the dirt off. It was a green ammunition box, like soldiers out in the field might use. "Perfect *stash* for a *cache*," I said to Dexter. He wasn't impressed with my rhyme.

I felt a charge of excitement that I'd found the geocache. But it had definitely been muggled, and that was really irritating to see with my own eyes. The lid wasn't fastened down right. When I opened the box, I saw that dirt and leaves had gotten inside. I pulled out the logbook and an empty plastic bag. The logbook should've been stored in the bag to keep it from getting wet or dirty. But other than that, there wasn't too much damage. It could've been worse. At least it hadn't gotten wet from rain.

I inspected the treasures inside. There were three more army men, one purple and one gold strand of beads, two rubber snakes, a small set of Allen wrenches, a little padlock and key, and a wooden nickel that said *Pinnacle Peak Patio* on it.

I smiled because that was a steakhouse in Scottsdale. Kendra, Shea, and I go there with Dad sometimes.

I took the wooden nickel, but the best treasure of all in the whole box was a duck call. I took it out and blew into it. It made a weird honking sound that I guess was sort of like a duck quacking. Dexter's ears shot up like a couple of antennas. He had such a surprised look on his face that I had to blow into it again. *Honk.* Up went the ears. Maybe just one more time. *Honk.* Boing! I cracked up over the way Dexter's ears moved every time I blew the call.

"Cool! A duck call, Dexter. In case we want to hunt wild

ducks sometime, huh?" I held out the little plastic mouth-piece for him to sniff. I definitely wanted to keep this treasure.

Then I slid my backpack off my shoulders and unzipped it to take out my treasures for exchange. That's the rule—you can take whatever items you want from a geocache as long as you leave something behind. I left a new red bandana in the ammo box. I figured bandanas were always a good thing to leave because you can do so many things with them when you're hiking—use them as a headband, make them into a sling, carry stuff in them, cover your neck when you start to get sunburned, whatever. I'd also brought a combination can opener/bottle opener/corkscrew. We sell about a thousand of these in the store every summer so it seemed like something people would find useful.

Then I took out the pencil stub and opened up the log-book, which was just a little spiral memo pad. I turned to the first page and saw that the first logged visit was last year on April 2, so this was still a fairly new geocache. Flipping through the pages, I noticed that quite a few people had found this cache over the summer—about nine different visits. Then I flipped to the end of the logs so I could record my find.

Except the last thing recorded wasn't a log.

It was a message.

HELP
WE NE

Help? Help Wene? What was that supposed to mean? I stared at the handwriting. It looked like some little kid had written it. Either that or someone trying to disguise their handwriting. All the letters were capitalized. Was this some kind of joke?

I sighed. Some kids must have done this—accidentally found the geocache, opened it up, scattered the toys around, and then left this stupid message.

But wait a second. What would kids be doing way out here? I looked around. We were miles from any houses, and we were 2.3 miles from the road. Maybe it wasn't kids. But I knew one thing: no geocaching parents would let their kids scatter the cache contents around and mess up the logbook. There were certain rules everyone followed. This was the first muggled cache I'd ever found. I was disgusted.

On the page right before the message, someone had logged this:

9/3—last day of the long weekend & we're heading back to Tempe in an hour. Our 3rd cache of the trip. Beautiful hike and great views! We hate to leave the mountains and go back to the desert heat. TNLN. Team Sparky

Okay, September 3. That was just last Monday—Labor Day—so the geocache had been muggled sometime during the past week. TNLN meant "took nothing, left nothing." Some people did geocaches just for the sport of finding them. I turned to the page after the scrawled message and logged my visit:

9/12—looks like cache was muggled. Lid not on tight, stuff scattered around, logbook out of the plastic. Cleaned it up. T wooden nickel & duck call. L bandana & bottle opener. C&D

"C&D" was for Chase and Dexter, of course. Then I cleaned out all the dirt and leaves in the ammo box, put the logbook and pencil stub in the plastic ziplock bag where they belonged, dusted off the AWOL army guy and his vehicle, and returned everything to the box. I made sure the lid was fastened tight to protect it from the elements before I buried it in the leaves inside the log.

We'd found our geocache, and it was still fun, even if it was a little muggled.

"Okay, Dexter. Let's go home."

But by the time we made it back to the road, I couldn't stop thinking. *HELP WENE.* Was Wene somebody's name? And why did they need help?

"Dexter," I called. He looked over his shoulder at me, his ears up.

"What if it isn't a joke?"

Chapter 2

When I got home, Rick and the girls were still at the store getting ready to close up, and Mom wasn't home yet. During the school year, she teaches a couple of business classes at Northland Pioneer College, so some days she doesn't get home until after dinner.

I went straight upstairs to the room we use as an office because I wanted to log my find on the geocaching website. It's so hard to get computer time in our house. Kendra and I fight over it all the time. She's sixteen, so she uses the excuse that she needs it for schoolwork. It's always, "I've got a paper to type," or "I need to do research for this report," but half the time I think she's just chatting with her friends.

Once I'd logged on to the website, I put down information that was basically the same as what I'd written in the log-book—that the geocache had been muggled and that I'd cleaned it up. Then I sat there with my fingers on the keyboard. Should I mention the help note?

I scrolled down to view the other logged visits to see if there was any record of anything out of the ordinary. People mostly made comments about what the weather was like when they found the geocache, or whether they had any trouble finding it, or if they'd seen any wildlife along the way. There wasn't anything unusual—no one saying they'd read any strange messages. So what should I do? Should I mention it?

I decided not to. It was probably just some non-geocachers who'd found the ammo box by accident.

This geocache was called "I don't know, but I've been told." It had a whole army theme, starting with the ammo box. According to the description on the website, the cache originally had some army men and a die-cast Jeep, dog tags, a couple of little GI Joe action figures, a camouflage cap, and three squirt guns. That was pretty cool, that it had a theme to it. Some caches do, some don't. It varies. It was fun to read all the logged visits and see what people took and what they left.

Then I checked my e-mail. Dad had sent me a message: "Mark your calendar!"

Chase—

How's school going? Hey, I've got a weekend planned for us in Nov. How's this sound? Fri. 11/2, you can come down for the weekend. I'll get tickets to the Suns game for that night. Against the Lakers, buddy!! And then Sun. afternoon on the 4th, there's an Open House at Brophy for 8th grade boys and parents. You need to see the place before you turn it down, Chase. Maybe your mom and Rick would like to come see the school too?

Sound good? I'll call your mom and make the plans. Oh, and it's just a boys' weekend. I'll pick up the girls for a weekend in Oct.
Love you,
Dad

I groaned out loud. "Dad, why do you do this to me?" I asked the screen. He knew he had me. Lure me in by getting tickets to a Phoenix Suns game and then, *oh, while you're in town, son, there just happens to be an Open House at Brophy.*

He'd been talking to me about Brophy all summer, hoping I'd want to go there next year instead of Round Valley High. But I've barely started eighth grade, so it seems weird to already be thinking about high school for next year.

A couple of years ago, Dad did the same thing with Kendra—tried to talk her into going to a high school in Phoenix. He just wonders if the schools up here are as good as the ones down there. But Kendra wouldn't even consider it.

At first I didn't like the idea of changing schools either. But then Dad showed me Brophy's website, and it did look kind of cool from the pictures.

But I don't know. Do I want to go to Brophy? It's a real hot-shot prep school so it would be really hard. And it's all guys. No girls for four whole years.

Not only that, it's in Phoenix, so I'd have to live with Dad, of course. Which would mean leaving Greer and living in the desert where it's hot pretty much year round, where it never snows and there are so many people.

But if I moved in with Dad, we could go to Suns games all the time, and Coyotes games too, although I don't like hockey as much as basketball. There's so much cool stuff to do in Phoenix. And it would just be us guys, which would be a lot of fun in some ways.

I barely even remember living with Mom and Dad together. They got divorced when I was five. Kendra was seven, and Shea was just a baby, hardly even walking, so she totally doesn't remember it. We lived in Mesa then, and I remember swimming in our pool. Pretty much everyone has a pool in the Phoenix Valley. And I remember how bright everything was, how the sun would blind me when I looked out the back door and all I could see was white stucco and blue pool water and sunshine. That's about all I remember.

Then when I was seven, Mom married Rick and we moved up here to the high country. Now it seems like I've lived here my whole life.

This summer, when the girls and I were at Dad's, he'd mentioned Brophy. "Look," he'd said, "I know your whole life is in Greer, and you probably don't want to move. But Brophy's a top-notch school. You'd get a great education. I'd love it if you or your sisters wanted to come back to the Valley for school. I miss you guys." Something about the way he said it really got to me. My chest felt all funny. He always says he misses us, but this time I heard it in his voice.

But I love living in the high country. I like watching the seasons change and seeing deer run through our backyard. I like having to put a brick on the garbage can lid to keep the raccoons out. I like my life the way it is.

I pushed the reply button and sat there with my fingers just touching the keyboard. I stared at the screen, trying to think of what to say. I wanted to tell him about how I'd figured out all the features of the GPS, and I was starting to get some use out of it. But I wasn't sure what I should say about Brophy.

Of course I'd come down for the weekend. No way would I pass up the Suns game, especially against the Lakers. And then we might as well go to the Open House too. My fingers twitched on the keyboard. Then I heard the door open, and the house got noisy.

"Chase?" yelled Rick.

"I'm in here!"

"Why don't you start a fire for us?"

"Okay!"

I hadn't noticed that while I was sitting in front of the computer, the room had gotten dark and the house was chilly. I exited out of my e-mail. I could write Dad later.

Chapter 3

That night I had trouble sleeping. And it wasn't from worrying about Brophy. Okay, maybe that was part of it.

Mostly I couldn't stop thinking about that message. *Help Wene.* The second word didn't make sense. Maybe it wasn't a word. Maybe they were going to write *we need.* If that was true, what did they need? And who were they? Somebody had been out there at the geocache in the past week, and they needed something. But what?

Maybe it was just a joke. But how could I know for sure?

There was really only one thing to do: go back as soon as possible and look around.

But the next afternoon Rick said he and Mom had some business to take care of, so that left us kids in charge of the store. I had to work, and there was no way I could get out of it.

Why did it have to be today that they needed us? I couldn't believe how bad their timing was. It didn't happen too often that Mom and Rick would both be gone. Business was always slow on a weekday afternoon in the fall, and Rick could've just closed up, but he hated doing that.

As it turned out, he might as well have closed the store. We had a grand total of four customers all afternoon. Mrs. McNary came by and rented a couple of DVDs. Rex Rutherford stopped and bought a cup of coffee and a newspaper and flirted with Kendra, which was pretty gross because he's got to be at least thirty-five. For the first time all afternoon, I was glad I was here to keep an eye on my sisters in case things got out of hand. Two other people we didn't know came in and bought a quart of motor oil, a Dr Pepper, and a bag of Cheetos. No wonder Mom and Rick called this the lean season.

Kendra and I were sitting on stools behind the counter with our books spread out in front of us. At least if I could get this math homework finished now, I wouldn't have to do it tonight.

"What do you suppose they're doing?" Kendra asked me. She'd been working on her chemistry homework, but she'd gotten bored and closed her book.

I shrugged. "I don't know." I glanced at the clock, wondering if I'd have a chance to get back to the geocache today. It was already ten till five. How much longer would we be stuck here? If they didn't get back soon, I could just forget about my plans. Kendra pulled her long hair back and piled it up on top of her head in a bun, then let it fall around her shoulders again. Her hair is dark brown and straight like Dad's, but Shea and I have light, wavy brown hair like Mom's. That's why I keep mine cut short. I hate how it curls.

This summer, I reached Kendra's height—5 foot 4—which was okay for a girl, but I hoped I'd be at least 6 feet eventually. Dad's 5 foot 11. My friend Chris is already 5 foot 9, and he won't be fourteen until February. I was really hoping I'd get a lot taller this year.

"Don't you think it's weird that they wouldn't even tell us

where they were going? 'We've got some business to take care of.' How vague is that?" Kendra looked at me with her eyebrows arched.

"So what are you saying?" I didn't like the way her voice sounded. It was like she was accusing our parents of some suspicious activity.

"I think I know what Rick's up to," she said with this real know-it-all tone. "I think he's looking for a job."

Shea was standing in the candy aisle organizing all the chocolate bars by wrapper color. Sometimes she does it alphabetically. "He already has a job. Why would he need another one?"

Kendra shook her head and gazed out the front windows. "Don't say anything, okay? I've got this bad feeling." She looked at both of us. "I heard them talking this morning before I got out of bed. About money. About how they didn't know how they were going to make it till ski season starts."

"Why would Mom go along with him if Rick had a job interview? Anyway, they're always like that this time of year. Every fall, they say they don't know how we'll survive. But we always do." I said this partly to reassure myself but also to reassure Shea, whose eyes widened as she listened to every word.

"No, it's not just that. They're really stressed about this. I could hear it in their voices." Kendra loves drama; she always tries to make everything seem like a big deal. Mom always says Kendra is destined for the stage, but this time I could tell she wasn't just being dramatic.

"It'll be okay," said Shea, turning back to the candy bars. "If Rick needs to get another job, then *we* can run the store. I'll be in charge of customer service. And inventory. But you two have to help me. Like right now, Chase could be stocking the paper products that just—"

"Shea, be quiet for a second, alright?" I looked at Kendra. "You're seriously worried about this, aren't you?"

Kendra pressed her lips into a thin line. "Yeah. Something's up. Can't you feel it?"

I couldn't really, but it didn't surprise me that Kendra could. She could read people that way. And if she felt like something was going on, she was probably right.

I wished she'd never even said anything. I had enough to worry about with Brophy. And now this. I turned back to my math book and forced myself to work five more problems. It kept me from having to think about all that stuff.

When Mom and Rick got home at a quarter to six, I was finally able to slip away and get on my bike. I could hardly wait to get back to see if there was anything new at the geocache site.

Today I had the advantage of knowing exactly where I was going. Dexter streaked ahead of me like a racehorse. He knew where we were going too.

Riding along, feeling the wind in my face, I felt like I could forget about everything. No school, no homework, no worries about what Kendra had just said. I was free. At least for a while.

It was just a little over five miles from my house to the geocache site, and yesterday it had taken me just under thirty minutes to get out there. I'd have to move faster today because I didn't have as much time before it got dark.

By the time we got to the fallen log, I was gasping for breath from the long ride uphill. I left my bike in the tall grass by the trees.

Okay. Now what? I looked around like I expected to see someone stuck up a tree or pinned under a rock or lying by the hiking trail with a broken leg—something obvious that would give me a chance to be the hero and come to some-one's rescue.

But there was nothing obvious. It was just Dexter and me all alone in the mountains with no sign of anyone needing help. Everything looked exactly the same as it did yesterday, except that the open meadow seemed faded and washed out in the late-afternoon light. All we could hear was the sound of the wind rustling the branches of the nearby trees.

I dug the ammo box out of the leaves in the log and opened it up to check the logbook. Everything was exactly the way I'd left it. No new entries, the logbook and pencil stub still in the ziplock bag, all the cache items still there.

Bummer. Maybe the note was just a joke after all. I was really hoping for something new. One more clue. One more piece of the puzzle for me to try to solve.

I looked around. Suddenly my back had a weird crawly feeling—like I could feel someone's eyes on me, watching me. I spun around. There was a grove of trees nearby, but I didn't see anything strange about them. Dexter was busy scratching his ear with his back leg. I knew there couldn't be anyone within a half mile of us, or he'd let me know.

I stood still, listening to the birds singing in the trees and the rustling of the leaves. The shadows were long here under the tree branches. Daylight was fading fast.

I flipped to the next-to-last page in the logbook and looked at the writing again.

HELP
WE NE

Now that I saw it again, I was sure that it was supposed to be WE NEED. There was a little space between the E and the N.

Maybe they'd been interrupted. They didn't have time to finish the message. That's why the lid wasn't on tight.

I took out the pencil and stared at the page. What should I say? Finally, I wrote this under the WE NE line.

What kind of help do you need?

Leave me a message. I'll help you if I can.

As I was putting the logbook and pencil back into the ziplock bag, my back felt all crawly again. Was someone watching me?

Dexter was inspecting the base of a tree. If there were anyone close by, he'd be barking. I looked up into the tree branches overhead. A sleepy raccoon might be watching us from its perch, but other than that, we had this side of the mountain to ourselves. I was just being paranoid.

But I kept looking at the trees, expecting…something. I shook myself, trying to get rid of that creepy-crawly feeling. Then I closed the lid of the ammo box and stuck it back inside the log, burying it under the leaves like I'd found it.

I spun around fast. Why did I keep having this feeling? I hadn't felt like this yesterday.

"Hey, let's do some exploring," I called to Dexter. He followed me into the trees near the fallen log and we crunched through the dried leaves. If anyone was around, they'd hear us coming. I wasn't sure what I was looking for. Just some…sign. Anything that looked like people had been here. We walked around for about twenty minutes, but we didn't see a thing.

When we got back to where I'd left my bike, I realized how late it was. I looked at my watch, and it was already 6:42. Then I took my GPS out of my backpack and turned it on. I checked to see what time the sun was supposed to set today. It said 6:28.

Hide and Seek

Great. The sun had already set and now I was almost out of daylight. I hopped on my bike and we took off. We had to get home as fast as we could. Once the sun goes down in the mountains, it's absolutely, totally, completely *dark*. There's not a single light anywhere. No streetlights, store lights, nothing. Just solid blackness. And I hadn't brought a flashlight. I'd forgotten that the days were already getting shorter, even if it was only mid-September.

I glanced around me and picked up speed. It almost felt like the darkness was creeping up behind us, about to swallow us whole. I pedaled with every ounce of strength I had, but going fast across the bumpy cinders jarred me so much I had to slow down a little so I didn't wipe out.

"Remind me to keep a flashlight in my backpack at all times," I told Dexter. My voice sounded high and thin. He ran ahead of me, a black smudge in the fading light.

Since we were heading east, what little light we had was to our backs. Pedaling away from the daylight into the growing darkness made it even harder to see. When we finally crossed the footbridge where the trailhead started, I let out a sigh. I felt slightly better that we were leaving the hiking trail and were back on a paved road. But the road was all tree-lined and woodsy, and that blocked out even more of the fading light. I pedaled as fast as I could. I was glad to at least be going downhill now. Dexter raced along beside me.

And then out of nowhere: a loud rustle in the leaves, a sudden movement, and right in front of us—a coyote! I braked and skidded to a stop. The coyote stood there looking at me. I was frozen in place, too stunned to move.

Then I heard a low, threatening growl. It took me a few seconds to realize it was coming from Dexter. In the shadowy darkness, the coyote bared its teeth and flattened its ears. Its bushy tail curled between its legs.

Pow! Dexter sprang toward the coyote with a ferocious bark. A flash of gray, and the coyote was gone. And Dexter after it! They tore through the brush at top speed.

The sounds of barking and snarling coming from the brush made my heart race. "Dexter! Dexter, come back here!"

My heart was pounding so hard it made my pulse throb in my throat. I gripped the handlebars of my bike and stared at the underbrush where Dexter had disappeared.

Could Dexter take on a coyote? He might get hurt!

"Dexter!" I yelled. My hands felt sweaty on the handlebars. There was nothing I could do! I couldn't follow them; the brush was too thick. Plus I could barely see a foot in front of me. The barking and snarling finally stopped. I swallowed hard and scanned the trees all around us. I kept quiet and listened for any sound, but it was hard to hear over my thumping heartbeat. "Dexter!" I whistled as loud as I could and slapped my thighs. "Come here! Come on, Dext!"

I listened. Nothing. I straddled my bike and propped my elbows on the handlebars, my legs jiggling with nervous energy.

"Dexter!" I called out in a high-pitched tone. "Come on! Let's go!"

I waited. Still nothing. I kept calling for what seemed like ten or fifteen minutes. Every minute that passed made me more and more worried.

Finally—*finally*—I heard leaves crunching. I squinted to try to see in the fading light. A dark form ran toward me from out of the brush. I tensed when I saw it—was it the coyote? But I could tell by the way it ran it was Dexter. He trotted up and bumped against my leg.

He was panting and wagging his tail. I could barely see his outline in the darkness. I let out a long, slow breath.

I laid my bike down and reached out to run my hands over him. Was he hurt? Did he have a bite someplace, or a scratch? That coyote could've been rabid. My whole body was trembling now, and I was glad to be squatting down because I suddenly felt too weak to stand.

"You scared me to death, stupid dog! You can't go chasing after coyotes." He seemed to be okay. He wagged his tail, head up, so proud of himself for chasing off that coyote.

"You stay close, alright?" I told him. "No more running off. We've got to go. We're already late." Even though he's a great dog and he's really smart, he does have this one bad habit: he doesn't always do what he's told. Especially if there's something interesting to chase.

My heart was beating normally now. But just because this wildlife encounter ended well didn't mean the next one would.

I should've known we might see a coyote. I've seen dozens, maybe even hundreds of them. It was the perfect time of day to see one too—just as it was getting dark. Or at night, crossing the road in front of the car, their eyes all shiny in the headlights.

We started down the road. It wasn't pitch-black yet but it sure was hard to see. I kept looking from side to side. No way did I want to encounter any more wild animals tonight.

It could've been worse. At least it wasn't a wolf. Or a whole pack of wolves. Mexican gray wolves have been reintroduced up near Big Lake. Even though I've never seen a wolf, sometimes late at night I've heard them. Howling way off in the distance.

We were getting closer to where all the cabins were, so I breathed a little easier. When we turned onto the 373, I wished for a few passing cars so we could see by their headlights, but there weren't any. By now it was so dark I was really straining to see in front of me. I knew we were on the highway—I could tell by the way the asphalt felt under my tires. I took out my GPS and turned on the backlight to give myself a little something to see by.

When we pulled into our driveway, all the windows of the house were lit up. I saw Mom standing in the doorway. Light from the kitchen made her nothing but a dark outline.

"Chase!" she yelled. "Where have you been?"

Chapter 4

"I know, Mom. I know," I said, hopping off my bike. "We were riding along near Sheep's Crossing and Dexter ran after a coyote. He just took off! I had to wait for him to come back. Sorry we're so late."

"A coyote?" she asked. "Is Dexter okay?"

"Oh yeah, he's fine. *I* almost had a heart attack, but *he's* absolutely fine."

"Well, you shouldn't be out after dark. Put your bike away and come eat dinner." I could tell she didn't know whether to be annoyed with me or relieved.

Inside, the house was all bright and warm, a stark contrast from being outside in the cool night air. I breathed in the delicious smell of Mom's homemade chili simmering in the Crock-Pot. The rest of the family was sitting around the dining table, halfway through their dinner.

"Where'd you go?" asked Shea accusingly. "Every day now you're always going off someplace." She gave me a look like she suspected I was up to something.

"Just out riding my bike. I spent all afternoon in the store—can't I get a little fresh air?" I didn't want the whole family to know about my little geocaching mystery. I wanted to keep it a secret, let it be something for me to do on my own.

"It's times like this I wish you kids all had cell phones," Mom said.

The problem with having cell phones in the high country is that you can't always get service. They work part of the time, depending on where you are when you call, but they're kind of unreliable up here in these remote mountains.

Rick looked at me. "Well, go ahead and get a fire started and then come sit down. Supper's waiting."

I let out a deep breath and went to the wood box in the living room. At least they didn't give me too hard of a time about being late.

I went to the side table by the fireplace and grabbed a handful of the junk mail that we always saved for kindling. Then I laid the fire and got the matches off the mantel. I have this little game where I try to see if I can start the fire and really keep it going with just one match, which is harder than it looks. This time, I really had to blow on it a lot in the beginning, and the smoke got in my eyes and made me cough. It took me three matches before I had a real blaze.

Dexter took a long drink out of his water dish in the kitchen and then went back out the dog door for his self-appointed guard duty. He'll stand out in the yard and keep watch till we make him come inside.

I took my empty bowl from the table and scooped out chili from the Crock-Pot. Mom was quizzing the girls and me about how much homework we had tonight when Rick interrupted her.

"Well, we had an interesting meeting this afternoon," he announced. We all stopped and stared at him. Mom had this knowing look. When I glanced at Kendra, she stepped on my foot under the table and raised her eyebrows at me.

"Yes, we did. Rick and I met with a real estate agent this afternoon," said Mom. She looked really serious.

Kendra shifted her eyes toward me for a half second and then looked back at Rick. "A real estate agent?" she asked. "Are we buying some land?"

"No," said Rick. He took a sip of water and cleared his throat. "Maybe selling the store and the cabins." Then he scratched his beard and kept quiet while we all sat there in shock.

"What?" Shea squealed. "You can't do that! You just can't!" Her spoon clanged against her bowl and she stared first at Mom, then at Rick.

Rick held his hands out like he was trying to calm her down. He's always very reasonable and rational about everything. "Hold on a second. We don't even know if we can sell them right now. It depends on if we can get a good price for them."

"If we sell the store and the cabins, where would we go?" asked Kendra, tucking a dark strand of hair behind her ear to keep it out of her face. Shea propped her chin on her folded hands, waiting.

Mom walked over and stood next to Rick. Obviously the two of them had been talking about all this for a while.

"Possibly back to the Valley," said Mom.

Then everyone was talking at once. Kendra wanted specifics—when, where, how, and why. Shea promised we'd work even harder in the store so they wouldn't have to sell it.

"When did you guys decide all this?" I yelled over the noise.

"Nothing is decided," Mom emphasized. "If we can't get a good price for the property, then we won't be able to sell. At least not right away."

"But we just can't go through another winter like we had last year," said Rick. "I don't know how we'd survive it."

That got everyone quiet. Last year we'd had a really bad winter. Bad meaning there was almost no snow.

Most winters we get lots of snow. And lots of snow means lots of tourists. All the people in the Phoenix Valley who want to get out of the heat during the summer also want to play in the snow during the winter.

They come up and go skiing at Sunrise, the resort just down the 260 from us. Or they go cross-country or rent snow-mobiles. Usually Sunrise opens early in December, or if it's a good year maybe in November. And then it stays open through March or April.

But last year there was hardly any snow. It got cold, but one sunny day came after another. The snow didn't fall, and our White Mountains were mostly brown.

The whole Southwest has been in the middle of a drought for a really long time, and last winter was one of the worst. Most people think Arizona's a desert, but only parts of it are. And having no snow isn't just about skiing. Having no snow is worse than having no rain. Snow takes its time melting, and water has a chance to seep down into the ground. That's better than heavy rain where the moisture just becomes runoff or evaporates. The melting snowpack in the high country helps the whole ecosystem. If there's no snow, animals don't have enough water, trees dry out and die, forest fires start. No snow affects just about everything.

But for us, not having much snow last year meant very few tourists. Which meant very little business during our second-busiest season. Our cabins sat empty all winter, and the local customers were the only thing that kept our store going.

We could always count on summers being hot in the Valley

and all the desert dwellers wanting to get away to the cool mountains. But last winter we found out we couldn't always count on snow.

I cleared my throat. "But this winter's supposed to be better," I said quietly. "El Niño's supposed to be back." That was a weather pattern I'd read about in the newspaper. In Arizona, it made us have wet winters. So there was more rain in the Valley and more snow in the high country.

"Maybe," said Rick. "But that's just a prediction."

"There are some advantages to going back to the Valley," said Mom. "You'd be closer to your dad. And there are good schools down there." She glanced at me with this bright look on her face and I knew she'd probably already talked to Dad about the Brophy Open House. He must've called her this morning.

My parents have the weirdest relationship. They act like old college buddies whenever they talk—like they just need to catch up on each other's news.

I used to wonder why they got a divorce if they got along so well. Kendra said I just didn't remember all the fights. She remembered that Mom and Dad drove each other crazy when they'd actually lived together. Anyway, Mom and Dad are so completely different, it's hard to imagine they were ever married. Dad is a total city guy who thinks staying in a hotel without wireless internet is roughing it.

If Dad thought it was a good idea for me to go to Brophy, he could probably talk Mom into it. But I had no idea Mom would consider making the whole family move.

"I don't want to move," I said, because I didn't. I really didn't. Even when I was thinking about maybe, possibly, going to Brophy, I just assumed Mom and Rick would still be up here in Greer. So at least I'd still have my summers and holidays in the mountains.

"We don't know for sure yet. We'll have to see what kind of offers we get," said Mom. She started clearing the table.

We all stood up and took our dishes to the sink and tried to act like it was a regular school night.

Nothing definite, they'd both said. If they'd announced it was a sure thing, at least I would know what was coming. This way I didn't know what to expect.

And in some ways that was worse.

Chapter 5

All the way home on the school bus, I stared out the window and thought about last night's conversation. Moving. We might actually be moving. I barely remembered what it had been like when we left Mesa and moved up here.

The way I saw things, I had the best of both worlds. I got to live in the mountains and spend all my free time outside by myself doing things I loved—mountain biking, fishing, exploring, and now geocaching. But I still got lots of chances to visit the city when we went to Dad's, and he always made sure to plan something fun—Diamondbacks or Suns games, the water park, museums, concerts, movies, restaurants. "A taste of culture and civilization," Dad called it.

If we moved, my whole world would be turned upside down. I'd be living somewhere in the Valley, probably in a house in the suburbs with a pool in the backyard. Maybe I'd go to Brophy. I'd be surrounded by culture and civilization. Our family would go camping in the high country a few weekends every year. Suddenly *we'd* be the tourists.

My best friend Chris leaned over my seat and smacked me on the shoulder. "You coming home with me or not?"

I turned around in the seat. "Uh, I don't think I can today."

"Oh, come on, man. You said that yesterday. You're avoiding me for some reason. Is it my body odor or what?"

That made me laugh. "Yeah, that's exactly it. Your body odor is keeping me away."

Chris could tell something was up, but I didn't want to get into the whole moving thing. I hadn't even told him about Brophy yet. Next year had seemed so far away.

I did feel kind of bad about not hanging out with him today. We hadn't done anything all week. But I had all this other stuff on my mind now. And anyway, I wanted to go back to the geocache site and see if anyone had answered my note.

"Well, what are you doing this weekend?" asked Chris. "Have Rick drive you over tomorrow so we can chill and play some Playstation. I'll make a point of showering. Maybe I'll even use deodorant."

"I gotta work tomorrow," I told him. "And basically every Saturday for the rest of my life. You could come help me stock shelves in the store," I suggested, knowing he'd never go for it.

"No, thanks. Don't your parents know about child labor laws?" The bus lurched to a stop and Chris jumped out of his seat, swinging his backpack over his shoulder. "Last chance. Coming with me?"

"Can't. Maybe next week."

"You're so lame, dude. See you later."

Dave Knowles, Kendra's new boyfriend as of this year, got off at the next stop, but not before they gave each other a quick smooch. If we moved, it would sure put a crimp in Kendra's love life.

The bus rumbled down the highway with only a handful of passengers left. I watched Carly Hudson, three seats ahead of me, talking to Joseph Hernandez. She couldn't seriously be interested in that guy, could she? I couldn't hear what they were talking about. I wondered if his throat closed up on him whenever he talked to her, the way mine did.

The bus dropped us off at the end of our long gravel driveway. Since it was Friday afternoon, Mom didn't have a class to teach today, so she'd be helping Rick out in the store. We had two cabins booked this weekend, and as soon as the girls and I got home, we had to do the checklist for the guests.

"I call driver!" yelled Shea as we dropped off our backpacks in the house and headed back out the door to go to the cabins.

"You drove last time," I reminded her. Shea loves driving the golf cart we use to transport stuff from cabin to cabin; I guess it makes her feel in charge.

"Oh, let her drive," said Kendra. "Let's just get this done fast."

We stopped by the store to say hi to Mom and Rick and to get the keys. Then we stopped at the utility shed to get the clean linens and supplies we needed.

"If we sell the cabins and move, we won't have all this work to do all the time," I said to Kendra. We both carried armloads of clean sheets and towels. Shea had run ahead of us and was climbing into the golf cart.

"Is that supposed to make me feel better? Because it doesn't. Do you realize how bad it'll be if we move? We'll become invisible."

"What do you mean, invisible?"

She shook her head and stared at the ground in front of us as we walked along. "I know everybody at my school. All the teachers, all the students, everybody. So do you. But if we transfer to some big high school in Phoenix or go to one of those private schools Dad's always talking about, we won't know anybody." She looked up at me and now she was really serious. "I'd rather be a big deal at a little high school than a nobody at some new school."

"Don't worry about it," I said. "Because you're not a big deal now."

It took Kendra about five seconds to get my joke, but by that time I'd run ahead of her and jumped into the golf cart. She scooted in beside me and smacked me on the shoulder. "Go ahead and laugh. But just wait. It'll be miserable."

"What will?" asked Shea.

"Nothing," I said. "Let's just get this done."

We bumped along the dirt road that led away from the store to where our cabins were hidden away in a grove of trees. According to our brochures and website, our cabins are "rustic, yet quaint." Guests are always commenting about the fresh scent of pine. It would be hard to get away from that smell, considering that the cabins are built out of pinewood and surrounded by pine trees, not to mention the pine needles scattered all over the ground.

Each one has a main room with a little living area, a small kitchen, and either two bedrooms or a bedroom and a loft. There's no TV or phone. All our guests have cell phones anyway, and some of them don't even mind that they can't always get service up here. For air conditioning, you open a window. For heat, you build a fire in the woodstove.

My sisters and I have perfected a system for prepping the cabins for guests. We could do this in total darkness with our eyes closed. The cabins are basically clean already because Mom and Rick clean everything right after the guests check out.

Kendra and I make the beds, and Shea puts out clean towels, little bars of wrapped soap, and toilet paper in the bathroom.

Hide and Seek

Then I load the wood box with a few pieces of firewood and some kindling. If guests need matches, we sell them in the store. While I'm doing that, Kendra sweeps away any dead bugs lying on their backs in the corners, and Shea holds the dustpan for her. We can have a whole cabin ready in under twenty minutes.

When we finished the first cabin, we moved on to the second. And then I was free, with the rest of the afternoon to myself.

I went home and grabbed my "outdoor" backpack that held all my necessary supplies. Then I hopped on my bike and whistled for Dexter.

We headed down the 373 in our usual direction. By now, Dexter acted like he knew exactly where we were going. I hoped there would be something new for me to investigate this time. Solving a mystery would cheer me up and keep my mind off the possibility of moving.

If there was nothing new going on, I'd definitely be disappointed. But if I didn't have a mystery to solve, maybe I could scout out a location for my own geocache. I liked the idea of picking my own hiding spot and choosing a container, then deciding what kinds of trinkets to put inside. Then I could put in the waypoints and come up with clues to put on the geocaching website. And every so often I could come back and check on my cache to see how many people had found it. That would be fun—to have my own little hidden treasure, and to see how many people could find it.

The weather was sunny, but it was a little breezy, which made all the leaves on the aspen trees flutter silver and green. Any time there's even a breath of wind, it'll send aspen leaves into a shimmering wave. The sky was a deep, clear blue, with big, billowy white clouds casting shadows on the ground as they scooted across the sky. The sun felt nice, but I could already feel a hint of coolness in the air. The mornings and evenings were definitely getting crisp these days. We'd built a fire in our fireplace practically every night for the last week.

As soon as Dexter and I got close to the fallen log, I looked around, wondering if I'd see anyone. As usual, the meadow was completely deserted. No sign of muggles, no sign of anyone needing help, not even a herd of elk this time.

I poked around inside the log with a stick to make sure there weren't any little critters in there before I reached in to pull out the ammo box. The dead leaves covering it up gave off a damp, earthy smell. The box was still latched tight, just like I'd left it yesterday, and all the contents were undisturbed. The logbook and pencil were still in the plastic bag.

Untouched. Nobody had been here.

I was so bummed. I went ahead and took the little memo pad out of the bag and flipped to the last page where I'd left my note.

I couldn't believe what I saw.

WE NEED FOOD

A charge ran through me like a jolt of electricity. I held the little pad in my hand and stared at the penciled message in front of me. *We need food.* Someone *had* been here! *We*—that meant at least two people. Or more. How cool! I was so excited to think that somebody was out here and they needed help.

All of a sudden, that crawly feeling washed over me again. Without a doubt, someone had been here in the past twenty-four hours. The evidence was right in front of me. My hands were actually shaking as I flipped to the first message I'd seen—the WE NE message. The letters looked the same, all capitals in a handwriting that could've been a kid's.

For a split second, I had an urge to jump on my bike and take off as fast as I could. It was creepy to think people had been here. Where were they now? Were they watching me? Were they hiding? Why would they be hiding? A hard shudder ran through me.

I slowly scanned the deserted meadow around me. Calm down. Wasn't this what I'd wanted? To come to someone's rescue? I drew in a long breath and stood up. Somebody needed my help. I could do this on my own. And if I couldn't help them, I could go get more help in town.

"Hello?" I yelled, startling Dexter with my sudden outburst. He perked up his ears and looked around.

"Is anyone there?" I yelled. I dropped the memo pad back into the ammo box and walked around, cupping my hands to my mouth and calling out. "Where are you?" I stopped to listen for a response. Nothing. "Are you lost?" I shouted. Dexter was anxiously looking about, trying to figure out what I was up to.

I left my bike lying in the grass since the terrain here was pretty rough for riding anyway. I walked through the grove of trees looking for any sign that people might have been here recently. My heart was pounding like crazy. I was half expecting to stumble across a dead body or something. I crept cautiously between the trees, trying not to make too much noise crunching through the groundcover. Dexter moved from tree to tree, sniffing them thoroughly before marking them as his own.

I started thinking about this documentary I'd seen on TV where a guy went out hiking by himself in the canyons of Utah and got his arm pinned under a huge rock when it slipped. He stayed there for days by himself, and no one knew where to find him because he hadn't told anyone where he was going. Eventually he had to cut his own arm off to free himself. Amazingly, the guy survived.

Maybe I'd find someone injured and I'd have to fashion a splint out of tree branches and strips of my T-shirt, which I'd rip into pieces. I tried to think of all the first aid I'd ever learned. *If the face is red, elevate the head. If the face is pale, elevate the tail.* I could do this, I kept telling myself. I could rescue someone if they needed it.

Or maybe someone was hiding, but they'd run out of food. Maybe it was a runaway, some kid—or kids, since the note had said *we.*

"Hello?" I waited for a response. "Anyone out here?" I could feel my pulse speeding up. I took a deep breath and let it out again. It was shady and cool among the trees and I stood still, listening. All I could hear were birds singing and the branches rustling overhead.

There was no one around. I was sure of that. The space out here was so open that I'd be able to hear voices from hundreds of yards away. Slowly, I made my way back to where I'd left the ammo box sitting out in the open with the lid unlatched. I picked up the logbook and flipped to the last page one more time. I stared at the message as if waiting for more instructions to appear.

I flipped through the entire logbook, looking for anything else that might tell me something. But except for the last pages which had the two mysterious messages and the one I'd written myself, there was nothing new.

I grabbed my backpack and unzipped it to see what I had inside to leave. I had my stainless steel water bottle that was about two-thirds of the way full, so I took that out. Then there was a sandwich bag full of trail mix and a package of beef jerky.

That was it. If I'd been going out for a long bike ride, I probably would've had a couple of protein bars with me and maybe an apple. Well, if these people really and truly needed food, some trail mix and jerky were better than nothing.

I looked at the ammo box with all its geocaching contents. I did *not* want to leave the food in there. There were certain rules that geocachers followed, and not leaving any food in a cache was one of them. Food would attract a lot more bugs and animals than it would geocachers, and the last thing you wanted was for a bear to find your geocache and help itself to a meal. A bear could peel back the top of this ammo box like opening up a pop-top.

I looked all around for someplace where I could leave this stuff. It wouldn't do any good to leave it on the ground or even on a rock. I had no doubt animals would get to it before the note writer would. If only I had a piece of rope, I could tie it to a tree branch or something. But I didn't.

And even if I did have a piece of rope, I doubted that tying it to a tree branch would really keep a hungry animal from getting to it. I'd have to leave the food hanging low enough so that the person could reach it, which would mean a lot of animals could reach it too. I bit my lip, trying to decide what to do. I really, really didn't want to leave the food in the ammo box. But there had to be exceptions to every rule. Somebody needed food. Wasn't that more important than maintaining a proper cache?

I put the package of beef jerky, the trail mix, and the water bottle inside the ammo box and flipped to the next blank page in the logbook.

This is all the food I have with me. I'll come back tomorrow (9/15) with more.

I paused, trying to decide what else I should write.

Are you lost? Do you need help? Leave more info so I can help you.

I stood there with the pencil hovering over the pad. What else should I say? What else could I do? I looked up to see if anyone was watching me. Dexter was lying in the grass, panting, his eyes half-closed against the afternoon sunlight. He was enjoying himself, at least.

I read over what I'd written and put the logbook back in the plastic bag. The clasps of the ammo-box lid made a loud metallic snap when I shut them, jarring the silence. Then I put the box inside the log and covered it up with dead, musty-smelling leaves.

There was no guarantee an animal wouldn't find it before the note writer did. But it was better than nothing. At least I'd tried. I wished I could stay and keep a lookout, but I had to get home before dark.

The good thing was I had the whole weekend ahead of me. "Let's go, Dext," I called and we started down the hiking trail. "You know what I think it's time for this weekend?" He trotted ahead of me, tail in the air. "I'm thinking it's time for a stakeout."

Chapter 6

At 6:34 the next morning, I heard the front door close as Rick left the house to go open the store by 7:00. Mom would be up soon making breakfast, so I had to do my kitchen raid now.

I threw my covers back and padded quietly across the floor to my bedroom door. I crept through the hallway to the stairs and down to the kitchen. The wooden floorboards groaned a little in certain spots, but I knew it wouldn't wake up the girls, and if Mom came downstairs, I'd just tell her I'd woken up early.

It was chilly downstairs. I shivered because I didn't have a shirt on, just pajama pants. All the curtains were drawn, and everything was quiet, like the house itself was still asleep, so I moved around carefully like I didn't want to wake it up. On the fireplace mantel, the clock ticked softly. In the shadowy darkness, I tiptoed over to the pantry and slipped inside, closing the door behind me and pulling the chain hanging down from the ceiling bulb.

The whole pantry lit up and I stared at the neatly organized shelves that went all the way up to the ceiling. We had all kinds of food, but some of it wasn't a good choice for my little mission.

For instance, there were probably about ten packages of ramen noodles and rows of soup cans, tomato sauce, and vegetables. But I couldn't take that stuff. I needed food you could eat right away that wouldn't have to be heated up.

Dry cereal? I could put some in a Baggie. Nah, that didn't fill you up. A can of tuna? But not everyone liked tuna. Shea couldn't even stand the smell of it, much less the taste.

What was I thinking? If they were starving in the woods, they'd be happy to have a can of tuna. But I kept looking.

Peanut butter. Perfect! Who didn't like peanut butter? Plus it was high in protein and it wouldn't spoil if it wasn't refrigerated. I grabbed the plastic jar off the shelf. I wanted to take some bread, too, but I knew that wouldn't keep for very long outside before it started to get moldy. I took a sleeve of saltines out of their box instead.

This wasn't a bad snack, but I wanted something more, so I also picked up a bag of almonds and a package of Pop-Tarts. Okay, not bad for the first kitchen raid. I opened the pantry door and pulled the chain to turn off the light. I heard the smack of Dexter's dog-door flap opening as he came in from outside to see who was awake. He brushed up against me, tail wagging. I could feel his hot, wet dog-breath on my leg.

"Hey, keep quiet, okay? Everyone else is still asleep," I whispered to him as I laid all my food out on the table. I opened the cabinet where all the plastic containers were and took out one to put the crackers in—so they wouldn't get crumbled to dust in my backpack. Then I found a big ziplock freezer bag and put the jar of peanut butter, the bag of almonds, and the Pop-Tarts inside and sealed everything up.

As I crept back up the stairs, I imagined Mom standing in the pantry, staring at the shelves and saying, "Didn't we have almost a full jar of peanut butter? Did those kids eat the whole thing in one weekend?"

It was a little sneaky taking food out of the pantry, but someone was out there in the wilderness, and they were hungry. They needed food, so why shouldn't I be the one to bring it to them?

When I got to my room, I closed the door behind me and stuffed the food supplies in my backpack. Then I crawled back in bed to get warm.

I hadn't planned on falling asleep again, but I must have because the next thing I remembered, Shea was bouncing on my bed.

"Wake up. Mom says there's two pieces of French toast with your name on them."

I rolled over. I'd definitely fallen back to sleep. "Stop bouncing. I'm getting seasick," I mumbled.

"You have to get up. We've got a lot of work to do today. There's still all that stock in the storeroom that hasn't been put away yet."

Shea was so into the store, she could be like a miniature Donald Trump sometimes, only with better hair. I rolled out of bed and pulled on a T-shirt before going down to the kitchen. Kendra was sitting at the table, her dark hair uncombed and falling all around her face. Mom was in front of the stove, watching the skillet. The kitchen smelled like coffee and breakfast.

I'd already thought of an excuse that would buy me a few hours of free time this morning. I just couldn't wait till Mom or Rick gave us a break sometime this afternoon; I wanted to get back out to the geocache site as soon as possible.

"Mom, did I mention that Jim Greenfield asked me to help

him chop firewood sometime?" I said, sliding into my chair and reaching for the syrup.

Mom looked over her shoulder at me. "No, you didn't mention that."

"Oh, maybe I told Rick about it. Anyway, he's going to pay me for it and everything. So would it be okay if I took the morning off from working in the store?"

I felt a bit of a twinge. It wasn't *exactly* a lie. Mr. Greenfield did ask me to help chop firewood, and he was going to pay me. We just hadn't decided on a date yet.

"That is so not fair!" Kendra protested. "You won't let me babysit for the Mitchells, but Chase gets to do all kinds of odd jobs." She glared at me.

Mom turned around with a spatula in her hand. "The problem with you babysitting for the Mitchells was getting you to Springerville and back. Chase can ride his bike over to the Greenfields'. Right?" She looked at me for support.

"Right. Anyway, it's not 'all kinds of odd jobs.' It's one job that will take up one morning," I told Kendra. I cut my French toast into a neat grid pattern and started eating. The bites were steaming hot, but I didn't care because they were swimming in melted butter and syrup.

"You know, that's just one of the drawbacks of living in such a remote area," Mom said, flipping a piece of toast. "You're both getting to an age where you might really like living in a big city. In the Valley, you both could get part-time jobs if you wanted."

"Oh, please! You can't make us fall for that. Look, it's not worth it to me or Chase to disrupt our whole lives and move. You haven't even asked us how we feel about it." Kendra shot me a quick glance.

Mom laid the spatula on the counter and turned around again to face us. "Fine. How do you feel about moving?"

"I hate it," said Kendra, staring past Mom's head out the window. "I do *not* want to move."

I thought about what Kendra had said yesterday—about becoming invisible in a big, new school. She'd obviously been thinking things through a lot more than I had. And even though I'd made a joke about it, I was kind of surprised that she sounded really scared about the idea of moving. She's always been good at making lots of friends.

Mom looked at me. "Your turn."

I kept stabbing one stray piece of French toast with my fork until it was full of about fifty little puncture marks. "I don't like the idea," I said finally. "But it's not like we get to decide."

What I wanted more than anything was for everybody to stop talking about all this. About moving. About me going to Brophy. When school started in August, everything had been normal. Now, all of a sudden, my whole life was about to change. I just didn't want to think about it.

Shea came in and stood with her face pressed against the kitchen doorframe. "What are you guys fighting about?"

"We're not fighting," Mom told her. She planted a stiff smile on her face.

"We're fighting about moving," said Kendra.

"Oh," said Shea, sliding into the kitchen chair beside me. "Well, I've been thinking about this. I have some ideas about how we can get more business."

Mom really smiled at that. "You do? Let's hear it."

"Well, first of all—the website. Let's face it. It's pretty blah. If we had a better website, it would bring in more guests for the cabins."

Mom nodded. "Well, that's a good idea. Look, we'll talk about all this later. I need to get to the store." She started loading the dishwasher and wiping off the counter. "How long will it take you to chop wood, Chase?"

"Um, I don't know. A few hours, I guess." I wanted to buy myself as much time as I possibly could.

"Well, no later than 12:30 or 1:00, okay? If you're not finished by then, tell Jim you'll come back another time to help him finish up. We need you in the store all afternoon. He'll understand."

"Okay, Mom. Thanks." I got up and put my plate in the dishwasher. All that talk of moving had turned the French toast to lead weights in my stomach.

I ran upstairs and got dressed, then walked through the house as casually as I could with my bulging backpack over my shoulder. I expected one of the nosy females in the family to grill me about why I needed my backpack to chop firewood, and what was in there anyway, but, surprisingly, nobody did. Maybe they didn't notice.

As soon as I was on my bike and speeding away, I felt this huge sense of relief. Escape! I was free. Dexter galloped along beside me, his ears flapping. I could tell he felt exactly the same way I did. I glanced at my watch and saw that it was ten after nine. That meant I had a good three hours on my own.

It wouldn't be an exaggeration to say that I'm happiest when I'm alone, riding my bike down some quiet country road. I felt the same way this morning that I did every time I got on my bike—like I could go anywhere I wanted to. I could ride this bike for miles and miles, only stopping to rest when I got tired. I loved the solitude, the feeling of breezing through space, pumping my legs with every ounce of energy I had, and then coasting along just from the momentum I'd built up. I

loved watching the trees speed by me in a blur or looking
down to see the dark asphalt of the road slipping by under
my wheels. But mostly I loved just being outside in the open
air, feeling the whole living, breathing world around me.

It was downright cold, probably still in the forties, and
pedaling at top speed with the wind blowing in my face made
it feel even colder. Pretty soon, my nose was stinging and my
eyes were watering, and I sort of wished I'd brought a pair of
gloves. I was glad I'd grabbed my Phoenix Suns cap out of my
closet at the last minute. At least my gray hooded sweatshirt
kept the chill off. Anyway, the sky was a beautiful clear blue,
so the sun would warm things up to the upper sixties by the
middle of the day.

When I pedaled past Jim Greenfield's house without stopping, I felt a little worried. I hoped he wouldn't happen to go
to the store this morning. Maybe I could still stop by his
house on my way home, if I had enough time. But for now, I
had another mission. I had a mystery that needed solving.

I couldn't wait to see what had happened at the site since
yesterday. Thinking about what I might find made me pedal
faster. When I got to the spot, everything looked exactly the
same as it had yesterday, but I went straight to the ammo box
and pulled it out. My fingers fumbled with the latches as I
opened it up.

The beef jerky and the trail mix were gone, but the water
bottle was still there. The note writers had found my food!
Awesome!

My pulse sped up as I opened the logbook to check for a
new message. But when I turned to the last page, all I saw was
the message I'd left the day before.

What? Nothing new—not even a thank you? I flipped
through all the blank pages in the memo pad to make sure I

wasn't overlooking something. Then I looked inside the ammo box for any sign of a note. Nothing.

I sat down in the dirt with the open ammo box beside me. I was hugely disappointed. How could someone who needed help take the food I'd left and not even bother to leave me a new note? What if this was some kind of joke? Maybe there was another geocacher out there somewhere, leaving me these notes and then laughing about it later. But who would do that?

Dexter came over and gave the open box a thorough sniff. "Who is it, Dexter? Is it the same muggles who were here before?"

I wondered what things smelled like to him—I knew he could still smell the beef jerky that had been left inside, because even I could smell that. I wondered if my smell was on this box along with the smell of anyone else who'd touched it.

If only I had a nose like that, it might help me solve this mystery.

I took my water bottle out of the box and stuffed it in my backpack. Whoever had taken the food didn't need water. That was very interesting. There wasn't a body of water close by. Why would anyone who was lost need food but not water?

Because maybe they weren't lost. They just needed food because...

"Hey! Where are you?" I yelled. Dexter looked at me expectantly. "Thanks for leaving me a note!"

I snapped the lid shut on the ammo box and shoved it back inside the log. Boy, this geocache had seen a lot of action in the past week. Then I took the bag of food out of my backpack. But this time I didn't bother to leave it in the ammo box. I looked around for a spot out in the open and decided to put the bag on a big rock so it could easily be seen.

"Come on, Dext. Let's get out of here," I said, but for some reason, I had this odd feeling like I was putting on an act for someone who might be watching me.

It wasn't the same as the other day when I'd had that creepy-crawly feeling of being watched. This time I felt like I was trying to trick someone who might be watching me into coming out and showing himself.

I took off without looking behind me. Dext and I headed in the same direction as usual, going east down the hiking trail toward Sheep's Crossing. But when we were a good three hundred feet away, I pulled over behind a stand of aspens and laid my bike down in the grass.

I glanced at my watch. Only 9:41. I had a few hours till I had to leave. Dexter wandered off to sniff around the nearby trees while I pulled my binoculars out of my backpack. I stretched out my stomach in the straw-colored grass and turned my Suns cap around backwards to get the bill out of the way. Then I focused on the rock where I'd left the food.

It was a perfect spot. Now all I had to do was watch and wait.

Chapter 7

Some people might've been bored, lying in the grass under some aspen trees, staring at a distant rock through binoculars for hours on end. But I couldn't have been happier.

I love being outside, breathing in the earthy smell of the ground, listening to birds chattering back and forth, feeling the sun grow warmer on my back. Mom, Rick, and Dad have all asked me at some point about what I want to be when I grow up. I'm not exactly sure, but I know I want to work outside. I think I'd suffocate if I had to sit inside a building at a desk all day. Rick said maybe I should work for the forest service, and that sounded like a pretty good idea. Or maybe I could work for a search-and-rescue team, finding lost hikers and stuff. That would be a pretty awesome job to have.

I propped up on my elbows and peered through my binoculars again. My little trick hadn't worked. If someone had been watching me at the geocache site, they were taking their sweet time retrieving the latest food stash I'd left for them.

I played around with the binoculars, focusing on different things. I watched a few birds in the trees and scanned the meadows for wildlife. I inspected the pale bark of the aspen trees and noticed that, almost overnight, quite a few of the little round leaves were starting to turn yellow. I zoomed in on Dexter's legs, examining the little leathery pads he had on his elbows. I rolled over on my back and looked up at the wispy strands of clouds in the blue sky visible between the tree branches. I checked my watch—11:09. I'd been waiting for almost two hours and still nothing. I decided I'd stick around till noon and then I'd have to leave.

I lay on my back staring up at the sky. The ground felt cold underneath me, and my left leg was starting to fall asleep. I had to keep jiggling it so it wouldn't go numb. I gazed at the endless blue overhead until I felt hypnotized.

A honking sound made me snap out of the daze I was in. I looked up to see a V of Canada geese flying in formation across the sky.

"Oh, cool!" I said out loud. "Look, Dexter. Geese migrating!" But he wouldn't look up. I was so glad I had my binoculars with me so I could watch them.

Sometimes I've seen them so high up they were just little specks in the sky, but this group was flying lower, maybe looking for a good place to land, and they were honking like crazy. I kept my binoculars on them until they were out of sight. But even after I couldn't see them anymore, I could still hear their honks in the distance.

I rolled over and focused on the rock again. Still nothing. But as I was scanning the surrounding trees with my binoculars, I caught a little movement. At first I thought it was a deer moving behind the trees. But then I saw a face!

Suddenly, Dexter sat up, his ears perked. In a flash he was on his feet, running and barking like a mad dog. I scrambled to grab my backpack and get on my bike to follow him. He raced ahead of me, and I bounced across the rough terrain as fast as I could, trying to keep up with him. He ran straight past the rock with the food, into the trees surrounding the fallen log.

This wasn't what I wanted to happen! I wanted to get a good look at who it was first, maybe be the watcher for a while instead of the watched. But this stupid dog gave me no choice. He was a real pain to have along on a stakeout!

By the time I caught up with him, his barking was constant. He'd found something. I heard a little noise—something between a yell and a gasp. As I came through the trees, there was Dexter standing in front of two kids, barking his head off.

They were both boys, and they looked pretty young. They also looked terrified. They stood absolutely frozen in front of Dexter.

"Dexter, come here! It's okay, don't be scared," I yelled to the boys. "He barks a lot, but he won't hurt you." When they saw me, they looked surprised, but neither one of them made a sound. They stood together, holding onto each other, looking like they were ready to take off running if either Dexter or I got too close to them.

"You surprised us," I told them. "We weren't expecting to see anybody out here."

Well, not totally true. I was *hoping* to see someone. So, were these my note writers? I glanced around nervously. Was anyone with them? It was a shock to have actually found real people after all that waiting.

They looked at me with huge eyes, still not moving. "It's okay. Really."

Dexter came over to me and I grabbed him by the muzzle. "No barking." He quieted down and paced around me in circles, keeping an eye on the kids.

58

Hide and Seek

"What are you guys doing way out here?" I asked, trying not to sound like I was accusing them of anything. I climbed off my bike and stood beside it, holding it.

The older boy looked at me and then looked at the younger one. His shoulder hitched up a little—a kind of half-shrug.

"Are you lost?" I asked. They looked awfully young to be a couple of runaways.

The older one shook his head. The younger one just stared at me. They were obviously brothers, they looked so much alike. Like a couple of bookends, just different sizes. They both had reddish blonde hair, the same turned-up nose, and a lot of freckles. They were wearing jeans and the same kind of pocket T-shirts. The little one was standing slightly behind the big one, holding onto the tail of his brother's T-shirt. He didn't take his eyes off me or Dexter.

"Are you out here all alone? Where are your parents?" I asked them. I hoped I sounded friendly. I didn't want to scare them.

The older one looked at his brother before he answered me. "We're camping."

"Oh. Where's your campsite?" I asked. I looked around but didn't see any sign of anyone camping nearby. And we weren't near any designated campgrounds.

Again he did that shoulder lift. He wasn't exactly a fountain of information. So then I thought of something.

"I brought you...I've got some food with me. You guys want a snack?"

They both nodded and stepped forward a little.

"Okay. Come with me. It's over here." I started pushing my bike as I led them over to the rock where I'd left the food. Dexter trotted just ahead of me, and the boys followed me, still keeping quiet. There was an awkward silence as the three of us walked along, and I kept glancing over my shoulder to make sure they didn't disappear into thin air. It still didn't seem real, but it was.

I'd found them! I'd actually found them! I was so excited I felt like jumping up and down and shouting. But I tried to act calm. I wondered if they realized how weird this whole situation was.

"I come out here to ride my bike and explore. A few days ago, I saw a herd of elk right over there." I pointed across the meadow. "I just saw some Canada geese flying south for the winter. They were honking like crazy. Did you guys hear them?" I asked over my shoulder. I was trying to make conversation so they'd feel comfortable with me.

The older kid shook his head.

"Too bad. It was pretty cool." When we got to the rock where I'd left the bag of food, I laid my bike down in the grass and slipped my backpack off my shoulders.

"Let's see what we got here," I said, as if I didn't know. I opened the bag and held it out for them to see. They walked up shyly and peeked in, like a couple of kids being offered treats from a bag of Halloween candy. "Peanut butter and crackers. Some almonds. And those are Pop-Tarts," I said, pointing to the silver wrapper. "What'll it be?"

"Pop-Tarts," said the little one in a croaky voice. It was the first time he'd spoken.

"Okay." I handed the silver package to the older one. "There are two inside—one for each of you. Hope you like strawberry."

I watched while the older one ripped open the shiny wrapper and handed one to his brother. Then they both bit into them and stood there chewing silently, like it was the most natural thing in the world for the two of them to be miles from anywhere, out in the middle of the woods eating Pop-Tarts.

While they ate, I got a closer look at them. They both had dirty faces, and their fingernails had a black line of grime under them, but otherwise they looked healthy and normal enough. The older one's jeans were way too short, and the little one's T-shirt was about two sizes too big. I also noticed that he had two different shoes on—one flip-flop, which was too big for him, and one Thomas-the-Tank-Engine slipper. If I had to guess their ages, I'd say the older one was close to Shea's age, about nine or ten, and the little one maybe seven or eight.

I felt so excited, like these two little kids had been lost in the wilderness for days, and now *I* was the one who had found them. I was coming to their rescue, giving them the food they'd been craving for days.

Once they'd finished off the Pop-Tarts, I took out the jar of peanut butter and the plastic box stuffed with crackers. I realized I hadn't packed a knife to spread the peanut butter with, so I retrieved my Swiss army knife from my backpack. Then I spread a big glob of peanut butter on several crackers, handing them off to each kid. They scarfed those down too. It made me happy to see they had a good appetite and they were enjoying all the food I'd brought. My snack selection had been a good one. Too bad I didn't need to administer any first aid.

"I'm Chase, by the way. And that's Dexter."

The older one nodded and didn't say anything. He was too busy chewing. When he'd had a chance to swallow, I asked them their names.

"I'm Jack. He's Sam," said the older one, pointing to his brother.

I handed them some more peanut butter crackers, eating a couple of them myself.

Now that I'd bribed them with food, I wanted some answers. I pulled the stainless steel water bottle out of my backpack and twisted the top off before handing it to Jack. I'd decided he was the spokesman for the two. "Where are you guys from?" I asked, still trying to sound casual and not like I was giving them the third degree.

Jack's eyes widened slightly and then he looked at me. "Arizona," he said, like he'd just come up with the right answer for a test question.

I couldn't keep from smiling. "Oh really? What a coincidence. I'm from Arizona too. Do you live in Phoenix?"

Jack nodded.

"Yeah, my dad lives in Phoenix. Actually Scottsdale. My sisters and I live up here in the high country with our mom and stepdad, but we go to the Valley a lot to visit him. What's the weather like down there now?"

"Cold," said Jack.

That made me burst out laughing. "Cold? Are you kidding me?"

The only time you could ever describe Phoenix weather as "cold" would be maybe one night in the middle of January when the temperature might dip into the thirties. This time of year it's still well over a hundred degrees down there. Even the lows are in the eighties.

Jack stopped eating and looked at the ground. I felt bad for embarrassing him. He cleared his throat. "Cold at night, I mean," he finally added without looking at me.

I figured he probably meant the nights up *here* were cold. That I could believe, especially if they were tent camping.

"So, where are your parents?" I asked. "You guys are kinda

young to be out here all alone." I wanted to interrogate them without making it seem like I was interrogating them.

Jack gave me a quick look. "We're not alone. Our dad's with us."

Sam nodded. He had a smear of peanut butter on the side of his mouth.

"Oh. The reason I ask is, someone left a note saying they needed food. I thought maybe somebody might be lost or in some kind of trouble," I said casually.

Sam and Jack looked at each other, and then they looked right at the log where the ammo box was hidden. I hadn't pointed to it or anything, so now I had no doubt I'd found the note writers.

"Do you guys know anything about that?" I asked, trying not to sound like I was accusing them. Jack looked back at the log but didn't say anything. Jeez, it was hard to get information out of these guys.

If Shea were in their place, she would've already offered up her entire life story. She was really outgoing with all our customers. But then, she was used to always having Mom or Rick around in the store with her. These kids were alone. Maybe it was a good thing they were a little suspicious of me.

"You want to see where I found the note?" I asked, and they nodded and started straight toward the log without even waiting for me. I tried not to let them see my smile.

I took them over to the log and poked around inside it with a stick. "To make sure there's nothing alive in there," I told them. "It's never a good idea to stick your hand in someplace you can't see."

I pulled the ammo box out and opened it up so they could see the contents. "It's a geocache," I explained. "See, some people hide containers with a few little items in them. Then they leave clues on a website for other people to try to find them. Once you find the cache, you can take something inside, as long as you leave something in exchange."

I pulled the logbook out of the ziplock bag. "And then the people who find the geocache record when they found it. It's just for fun. Kind of like a treasure-hunting game." I flipped through the pages of the memo pad, and Jack watched me and nodded like he knew all about geocaches.

"We thought people hid food in there," said Jack.

"Yeah, one day we saw people—"

Jack gave Sam a warning look that made him clamp his mouth shut.

So they'd seen the last geocachers before me, huh? That explained how they'd found it hidden in the log.

Now Sam was peeking inside the box as if he was looking for more snacks. Inside were the strings of beads, the bandana, the miniature padlock and key, the can opener, the wrenches, the rubber snakes, the army men and toy Jeep. But no food.

"Nope, you can't put food in here because out in the wilderness, animals and bugs are probably going to find it before people will, even if it's in a container like this. But I did leave some food in it yesterday."

"We found it," said Jack.

"Well, from now on, I won't leave any more food in there, okay?" I said. I was trying to carefully work the conversation around to why they needed food in the first place.

"I like these guys," said Sam, reaching into the box and pulling out a couple of the green plastic army men.

"Put 'em back," whispered Jack. "They're not yours."

Sam clutched the army men in his fist and looked up at

me to see what I would say about it. Was I going to get onto him like a grown-up or let him play with the army men?

"It's okay. You can keep them if you want, but if we take something, we have to leave something." I walked over to where I'd left my backpack and looked through it. I still had the wooden nickel in the front pocket, so I grabbed that.

"Here. You guys can each take an army man and we'll leave this wooden nickel for exchange." I held the nickel out for them to see and then put it back in the box.

Sam looked at Jack to see if that would be okay. Jack nodded, and Sam solemnly handed him one of his army men. "But don't let Dad see them," Jack whispered to his little brother.

"Okay, I'll keep it in here," Sam whispered back, stuffing the plastic figure in the front pocket of his jeans.

I got a kick out of the way they whispered to each other as if I couldn't hear them. I could tell they were nice, polite kids.

"So where's your dad now?" I asked as I snapped the lid of the ammo box shut and put it back inside the log.

Jack and Sam looked at each other. "Sleeping," said Jack.

I nodded. "At your campsite, I guess, huh? Yeah, lots of people go camping up here, especially in the summer. Are you guys tent camping or do you have an RV?"

Jack's shoulder went up again—that little half-shrug. I couldn't tell if he did that when he didn't know the answer to a question or when he just didn't want to tell me.

"Got any more food?" asked Sam, looking at the rock where we'd left our little picnic.

"Sure. There are a few more crackers, and a bag of almonds." I walked over to retrieve the plastic bag. "You like almonds?" I tore the package open and shook a few out in my hand for them. The two of them reminded me of a couple of little fawns that I was trying to coax with food so I could get a closer look at them.

Sam walked slowly up to me, gazing at the nuts in my hand. "I *think* I like almonds," he said shyly before picking one up and putting it in his mouth. He chewed thoughtfully and then nodded. "Yeah. I like almonds." He reached for a few more.

I handed the bag to Jack. "Go ahead. You can have the whole bag. You guys aren't the only ones who get hungry when you go camping. My parents own a store in town, and campers are always coming in to buy food they forgot. I guess your dad didn't bring along a lot of food, huh?" A plan was starting to come to me.

Jack glanced at me. "We have *some* food."

"Oh, I'm sure you do. Everyone takes some food when they go camping," I assured him. "But you could probably use some more, huh? Want me to bring you some more snacks tomorrow?" I was pretty sure they'd go for this bait.

Sam broke into a grin. "Yes, please!" I noticed that both of his front teeth were just growing in, one a little ahead of the other one.

I smiled back at him. "What's your favorite food?"

"Candy!" said Sam.

"Pizza," said Jack. "And hot dogs."

I laughed. "Okay. I'll try to bring some good stuff." Now it was time to make my big move. "Let's go to your campsite so I'll know where to find you tomorrow."

Jack and Sam exchanged quick looks. Neither of them moved.

"I can definitely bring candy, and I'll try to bring pizza.

Maybe even a few more surprises." I hoped the more I talked about food, the more they'd open up to me.

Jack looked at me as if he was seeing me for the first time. "You're not a cop, are you?"

I clenched my teeth together to keep from laughing. "No, I'm only fourteen," I said. "I'm not old enough to be a cop." He looked at me closely and I pulled my Suns cap off and held my hands out, palms open, for him to look me over. "I'm just a kid like you. Only older." So they didn't like cops, huh? Very, very interesting.

"Are you a snoop?" asked Sam.

At first the question caught me totally off guard, but I could see they were both waiting for my answer. So I shook my head quickly. "No, I'm not a snoop, either. Just a kid on a bike."

"My dad doesn't like snoops," said Sam, biting an almond in half between his side teeth.

"Me neither," I assured him. "I hate snoops. They're so… snoopy."

That made them both laugh, and I laughed too. Whatever I could do to get them to trust me. I had no idea what these kids' story was, but now I was dying to find out. Were they really camping with their dad? Somehow I doubted these were the typical weekend campers who came in our store to buy Jiffy Pop.

"So let's go see where your campsite is." I nodded at Jack. "You lead the way, buddy."

Jack stood still. I could practically see the wheels in his brain spinning. "But my dad's asleep right now."

"Yeah, he stays up at night to keep a lookout," Sam added.

A lookout? A lookout for what? Or for who?

"Oh, no problem. We'll be really quiet. We'll whisper," I murmured to him, holding my finger up to my lips. "I promise we won't wake him up."

Jack and Sam looked at each other. Sam cupped his hand over his mouth and whispered in Jack's ear and then Jack whispered something back. So many secrets for such little kids.

Jack looked at me. "Okay," he whispered. "But be very, very quiet."

Chapter 8

I left my bike and my backpack near the geocache, but I made a point of taking my GPS out first and turning it on. I went to the geocache waypoint I'd marked before slipping it back into the pocket of my cargo shorts. I wanted to figure out where their campsite was in relation to the fallen log.

Jack led the way through the trees. Even though most of the area was open meadow, there were a few trees nearby, and we stayed among those, either for cover or because this was the way Jack knew to go. Sam walked behind him and every now and then glanced over his shoulder at me to make sure I was still following along. When I smiled at him, he'd smile back, showing his uneven front teeth. Dexter walked near me, but mostly he followed a scent trail he'd discovered and found interesting.

I pulled the GPS out for a quick look. We were now 426 feet away from the geocache waypoint, going northwest.

We came out of the trees and into the open again, with meadows in front of us. I looked behind us, and even though we hadn't gone that far, I couldn't see where I'd left my bike because the trees obscured the view. I realized someone could be really close by and still watch the cache site without anyone knowing it. Had these kids been watching me from here?

We walked along in a kind of shallow wash, and I could see that it was leading us into another stand of juniper trees up ahead. Through the trees, the outline of a white pickup truck with a camper on top was just visible. I could also see a tent nearby.

Jack stopped short about two hundred feet from the campsite and glanced at Dexter who was sniffing the base of a tree. "We better not go any closer," he whispered. "Dad doesn't like for us to make noise when he's sleeping."

"Okay," I whispered back. "So that's your campsite?" Jack and Sam nodded.

We'd come .29 miles northwest from the geocache waypoint. I marked this spot as a new waypoint before slipping the GPS back in my pocket. Sam and Jack watched me silently but didn't question what I was doing.

Then I motioned for them to follow me back the way we'd come, creeping along quietly to show them I respected their need for secrecy. When we were back under the cover of the trees, I stopped.

"Okay, now I'll be able to find you again tomorrow when I bring the food."

They both gazed at me with wide eyes.

"You do want me to bring more snacks tomorrow, don't you?" I asked, crouching down so I was looking at them on their level.

The boys nodded. "Candy," Sam reminded me.

"You bet I'll bring candy," I said, giving him a playful punch on the shoulder. "And pizza, and some surprises."

"What kind of surprises?" asked Sam.

Hide and Seek

"I can't tell you or it wouldn't be a surprise, right? But it'll be something good, okay?" I smiled at both of them. A thought flickered through my head. I pictured myself at about their age and Mom lecturing me about not talking to strangers—*don't ever take food from strangers, or get in their car, or follow them anywhere or…*

A sudden wave of guilt washed over me, because I was absolutely using food to win their trust. It was so easy too, even with Jack's caution.

But they can trust *me*, I told myself. I wasn't going to hurt them. I wanted to help them. Something was definitely up with these little guys, wandering around up here while their dad slept. Were they really camping? Then why were they so hungry? And secretive?

The two sat down beside me, and Sam pulled his army man out of his pocket and made him skip through the dirt. I noticed both kids had a strange smell, not really body odor— they were too young for that—but something else. A slightly cheesy smell, like they hadn't had a bath in a while. Their thin arms poked out of the sleeves of their T-shirts, and their clothes were all dusty. But basically they looked like pretty normal kids.

Dexter was scratching his ear with his back leg, and Sam watched and giggled. He called Dexter over to him, and Dexter let him scratch him behind the ears.

"You'll still be here tomorrow, right?" I asked. "Tomorrow's Sunday. What day are you going home?"

"We've been camping a real long time," Sam offered, and Jack shot him a quick look, like he was giving out too much information.

In the fall, usually families who came up to the mountains

to camp out would arrive Friday evening and leave sometime in the afternoon on Sunday so the kids could go to school and the parents could go to work on Monday.

"But don't you have school this week? What grade are you guys in?" I asked.

They gave each other what I now thought of as "the brother look"—a silent communication that seemed to say a lot more than I could figure out.

"What grade are *you* in?" asked Sam, pointing the tip of the army man's plastic rifle at an ant crawling in the dirt. He even made shooting sound effects like I used to when I was a little kid.

"Eighth grade. Let me guess. I'd say you were in fourth grade," I said, pointing to Jack, "and you're in second grade," I told Sam.

"I'm in kindergarten," said Sam, not looking up from the army man. Jack's eyes darted from Sam back to me.

There was no way this kid could still be in kindergarten. He looked a lot closer to seven than five. Like his front teeth, for one thing. Didn't kids start getting their permanent teeth when they were older than five? At least the front ones, anyway? I don't know—maybe it could happen. I didn't let on about my suspicions.

"So was I right, Jack? You're a fourth grader this year?" I pressed.

Jack nodded. "Yeah. Fourth."

No way. No way were these guys four years apart in age. Two years was my guess—three at the most. The more information I got from them, the stranger this all seemed to me.

"But we don't go to school," said Sam. He shook his head and dragged his soldier along bumpy terrain. "Not anymore."

Jack glanced sideways at me to see how I would react to this information. I just nodded matter-of-factly.

"Oh, you're probably home-schooled then. You don't go to a regular school with other kids but your parents teach you at home?"

Jack nodded eagerly. "Yeah. Home-schooled." A look of relief spread across his face. He seemed glad to have a new name to put to it.

I glanced at my watch and was stunned to see that it was already 12:43. I'd told Mom I would be at the store by one o'clock at the latest.

"Hey guys, I have to go home now," I said. "But I promise I'll come back tomorrow and bring some food if you want me to." I stood up to leave.

"And some surprises too," Sam reminded me.

"Sure. Some surprises too. What time do you want me to meet you?" I glanced over in the direction of the campsite. "I'll come at a time when your dad's asleep," I whispered. If they were going to be so secretive, I would be too.

Jack gave Sam the brother look. "He sleeps during the day," he said.

"All day? You want me to come at this time tomorrow?"

Jack and Sam looked at each other and nodded.

"Okay. Tomorrow sometime between twelve and one o'clock," I said. Then it occurred to me that they probably had no idea what time that was. "In the middle part of the day. When the sunlight looks the way it does now," I said. "Where do you want to meet?"

Jack jerked his head in the direction of our first meeting place. "Over there. By the log."

"Okay. I'll see you there tomorrow in the middle part of

the day. But if you're not there, I'll try to wait around for a while. I'll only come over here if I don't see you."

A sudden look of fear spread over Jack's face.

"Don't worry—I won't come near the campsite. I won't let your dad see me," I assured him, because I knew that was what he was afraid of. "And if I don't get a chance to see you, I'll leave the food in the box. But you gotta try to get to it tomorrow, or"—I almost said *a bear* but then thought better of it—"a raccoon might find it first. You don't want a raccoon to eat your candy, do you?" I asked Sam in a teasing voice.

Sam shook his head and grinned at me.

I smacked my leg and Dexter stood up and shook himself. "Okay then. See you guys tomorrow."

The two boys waved and headed toward the edge of the clearing. I waited until they were out of sight, and then rode off as fast as I could. Amazing! I'd actually found my note writers, and now they really did need my help!

At least it seemed like they did. "Dexter, there's something weird about those kids, right?" He gave me a quick look as he ran along beside me, panting.

I wasn't just imagining things, was I? It's not weird to be camping, but what was up with their dad sleeping during the day and keeping a lookout at night? And why did they act scared of him?

My bike bumped along through the cinders scattered across the hiking trail. Was I interfering by giving them food? But that's what the note said they needed. If they were just on a camping trip, why were they so hungry?

It seemed like now that I'd actually found the note writers, I had even more questions than before.

Chapter 9

Sunday morning I volunteered to stay behind and help Rick while Mom and the girls went into Springerville. Sunday might be a day of rest for a lot of people, but not if you're in the tourist industry. It was our second-busiest day of the week. To make up for it, we always had "family time" on Sunday nights.

The guests had just checked out of Cabin 2, so I had to take the sheets off the beds, grab the dirty towels, and empty the trash cans. And since they'd had a fire in the wood-burning stove, I had to scoop out all the ashes. What a pain. At least I didn't have to clean the kitchen and bathrooms because Mom and Rick would do those later. I locked up and went into the store to drop the key off with Rick.

"What about Cabin 1?" I asked. "Want me to do that one too?"

"Guests haven't checked out yet. Should be out by 12:30. They asked if they could stay a little later. Let the girls take care of it when they get back."

I went to the freezer and pulled out a package of mini frozen pizzas. "Mind if I take these for lunch?" I asked.

"Don't we have food at home you can eat?" he asked.

"Yeah, but I'm really craving pizza."

"Fine. I'll mark it down. Go take a little break. You've earned it."

When he said that, I cringed a little inside. I still felt guilty about my bogus firewood-chopping excuse. When I'd finally arrived at the store yesterday afternoon, I was panting and sweaty from the long five-mile bike ride at full speed. Mom had fussed over me, saying I'd worn myself out working for Jim Greenfield all morning.

"How much did he pay you?" she'd asked. I'd told her we weren't finished yet and I'd have to go back some other time.

"I hope your hands didn't get blistered from swinging an ax all morning."

"They didn't."

My answers to Mom's questions reminded me of Jack's—short, not giving away any more than he had to. It must be hard for such a little kid to keep secrets.

And now I had secrets too. I hadn't mentioned that I'd met a couple of kids out in the wilderness. The whole thing still seemed suspicious to me, but I didn't say anything to Mom or Rick. Maybe the boys and their dad were just camping. Or maybe there was more to it. I figured the only way I could find out would be to spend a little more time with them.

"Hey, I'm going out on my bike for a while after lunch, okay?" I asked Rick.

"Yeah, okay. Just be home before dark so you don't worry your mom. The other night she was sure you'd had a wreck or blown a tire or something and you were stranded all alone somewhere."

I rolled my eyes. "I've got Dexter with me, and my GPS. What more do I need?"

Rick nodded like he wasn't the one who worried about me.

"I know. You need your freedom. I was the same way when I was your age. I'd go camp out by myself and fish and hunt for a week at a time during the summer."

"Really? You did that when you were *my* age?" Mom would freak if I ever asked to spend a week alone camping out.

"Well, maybe I was a little older. Fourteen or fifteen. I know I was doing it before I could drive, because the summer I got my license I drove up to Yosemite and spent two months up there in this old '79 Chevy pickup I'd bought and rebuilt the engine on."

Hearing that story made me feel like I was still in grade school. Rick's always been really independent. He can fix anything that's broken, he's strong as a mule, and as far as I can tell, he's not afraid of anyone or anything. Would I ever be that kind of guy when I was grown up?

"When did you feel like…like you were finally grown up? Like, okay, I'm a man now because I can…drive or…I have a job or…whatever?"

Rick looked thoughtful as he scratched his beard; then he gave me this sort of half-smile. "I'll tell you what made me feel like a man. The summer I was nineteen, a buddy and I worked for his father roofing houses. Whew! That's the most back-breaking work I've ever done." Rick chuckled and nodded. "Roofing houses—that'll make a man of you."

I figured I'd pass on the roofing houses part. "You know, it's only two more years till I get my driver's license."

"Yep, you've got lots of milestones ahead of you, Chase. Getting your license, graduating from high school. College. A job. All those rites of passage that everyone goes through."

"I guess. All that feels like it's a long way off."

"I know. Time moves slow at your age. But it'll happen."

Neither one of us said anything after that. I liked talking

to Rick about stuff like this, but I kind of wanted to get away and check on Jack and Sam.

I made a little coughing sound and asked, "Anything else you need me to do?"

No, you can take off. Just be home before dark," Rick reminded me.

When I got to the house, I went into the kitchen to cook the mini pizzas. The first thing I noticed was a business card and some papers on the counter. I recognized the lady's picture on the card as the person who had come to the store yesterday afternoon to say hi to Mom and Rick. The three of them had gone outside and walked around. And talked and talked and talked.

"That's the real estate agent," Kendra had whispered as we watched them through the store windows.

"How do you know?" I'd asked.

"Can't you tell?"

I don't know what they talked about but, whatever it was, it sure took them a long time to cover everything they wanted to say to each other. Mom and Rick showed her our house, the store, the cabins, and then the three of them stood outside as the sun set and yakked their heads off for an hour.

But after the lady left and we closed up the store and went home for dinner, Mom and Rick hadn't mentioned a word about their little meeting. And the three of us sure didn't bring it up.

I popped the little pizzas into the oven and set the timer, then went upstairs to get the other stuff. The night before I'd stashed some candy in my backpack along with a metal tackle box which had the surprise for Jack and Sam inside. I couldn't wait to show it to them. Then I took my backpack downstairs and got Dexter's leash and a rawhide, in case I needed them.

Hide and Seek

When the pizzas were done, I let them cool for a few minutes, then wrapped them in aluminum foil. I grabbed three pineapple raisin muffins from the tin on the counter and stuffed them in a Baggie. The last things I packed were two stainless steel water bottles. I slung the heavy backpack onto my shoulders and went outside. Once I was on my bike, I whistled for Dexter, and we took off.

By the time I got out to the geocache site, it was 12:15. I walked around and kept an eye out, but the boys weren't anywhere near the log.

I decided to go looking for them. But first I had to take care of Dexter. I couldn't trust him not to run off and start barking if he saw something. "Come here, Dext," I called to him. After I'd given him a thorough ear rub, I snapped his leash to his collar, then tied the other end around the trunk of a thin aspen. And since I knew he wouldn't like being left behind, I pulled the rawhide from my backpack.

"Look, a chewy!" His tail wagged and he took it from me. Then he settled down in the dry grass to start gnawing away.

I left my bike nearby but kept my backpack on me. I followed the same path we'd taken yesterday through the trees to the wash until the campsite was in view.

Except this morning, the white pickup was gone. I pulled out my binoculars and zoomed in on the scene. Through the trees, I could still see the tent, so they hadn't packed up and left entirely. But I didn't see any sign of them. I decided to take a closer look.

I crossed the meadow to the stand of trees, keeping my eye out for the white truck. About a quarter of a mile away off to the north was the road to Big Lake. That had to be the way they'd come in. I felt pretty sure I'd hear their truck and could get out of sight before they saw me.

Once I was in among the trees, I crept up to the little clearing where their campsite was hidden away. They'd set up camp there on a patch of hard-packed dirt. Besides the tent, they had a camp chair, a folding table, and a cooler. As I opened the lid, the stink of old fish hit me, but it was empty. There was a Coleman stove on the folding table. Sitting on top of it was a pot with what looked like leftover beans inside. On the ground was a plastic tub full of clean pots and pans. A collapsible plastic jug held water, and a couple of blue tin cups were upside down on top of it. A black, half-filled garbage bag hung from a piece of rope tied over a tree branch. A few yards away among the trees I saw a piece of burlap fastened around four poles. Their latrine, I figured.

The flaps of the tent were open, so I peeked inside. A bunch of rumpled sleeping bags and blankets covered two air mattresses. In one corner was a red milk crate stuffed full of clothing. The inside of the tent smelled musty and warm. It was definitely big enough for three people, though, especially if two of them were kids.

I hate snoops. They're so...snoopy.

That's what I felt like, creeping around and checking stuff out. What would their dad do if they pulled up right now and caught me?

There wasn't anything out of the ordinary here—just a typical campsite. I slipped away, not wanting to hang around there any longer than I had to. I crossed the meadow and walked up the wash till I was about two hundred feet away, under the cover of the trees. Then I stretched out on my stomach to wait and watch.

I was a little concerned about leaving Dexter alone, but so far he hadn't made a sound. I hoped his rawhide would keep him occupied for a while.

Hide and Seek

I'd been waiting about twenty minutes when I saw the white pickup with the camper approaching on the road to Big Lake. It turned off and bounced across the grassy field, coming to a stop under the trees next to the campsite. I pulled my binoculars out of my backpack and focused in, pushing my cap off so I could see.

The truck had an Arizona plate on it, so they really were from somewhere in the state, like Jack had said. Through the driver's open window I could see a man with red hair and a growth of beard. Inside the cab next to him were Jack and Sam; Sam's head was just visible over the dashboard. A rifle was in a gun rack on the back window of the cab.

When the man parked the truck and got out, I noticed he wasn't very tall, maybe five foot six, but he had muscular arms and a broad chest. He was covered in freckles, not just his face but his bare arms too.

The apple doesn't fall far from the tree. That was an expression Mom used when she was commenting on how much I reminded her of Dad. Even though I think Kendra looks the most like Dad, Mom's always telling me that I'm the one who favors him. "You stand like your dad. You walk like your dad. Even your voice sounds like his."

Looking at this guy through the binoculars, I had no doubt Jack and Sam fell from his tree. There was definitely a family resemblance. It made me wonder what the mom looked like.

As I watched them, I could see that the three of them weren't talking much, but there was a kind of unspoken communication among them. Each one of them seemed to know what to do. Jack and Sam climbed out of the truck and went around to the tailgate. Jack pulled the latch and they reached inside, pulling out a string of trout—three of them. Not bad for a morning's catch.

They took the fish over to the cooler where the dad had taken out a knife. He cleaned the fish while Jack and Sam climbed back into the camper of the truck. They came out clutching some cans to their chest. I watched the dad nod and say something to the boys, and then Jack fished around in the plastic bin full of clean pots and took out a can opener. When the dad finished cleaning the fish, he started up the Coleman stove.

They looked just like any other family camping out in the woods and preparing a meal. He wasn't yelling at the boys or smacking them around, and they didn't act like they were afraid of him. And even though they'd scarfed down the food I gave them, he was obviously feeding them. I'd been really suspicious yesterday, when they'd been so nervous about letting me get close to their campsite and so worried about waking up their dad.

All sorts of crazy ideas had gone through my mind yesterday about how maybe these kids had been kidnapped, or maybe the father they talked about was drunk or mean or something. He was letting his poor kids go hungry and wander around unsupervised. I'd even formed a little plan of sneaking them away from him and hiding them in one of our cabins all winter, bringing them food when they needed it and keeping them safe.

But maybe there wasn't anything unusual about this family. Maybe they were just camping out, like Jack said. Okay, so they didn't go to school, they were kind of grubby, a little hungry, and dressed like hobos. That didn't mean they were in any kind of trouble.

I scanned the three of them with my binoculars. Maybe they were homeless. Maybe this was just a family who'd fallen on hard times, and the dad was doing his best to take care of his kids. I wondered about the mom. Neither one of the kids had mentioned her.

If they were homeless, maybe I could help them out—bring them food and blankets and other stuff they might need. Why couldn't the whole family stay in one of our empty cabins for the winter? They'd be warm at least, and they'd have a little kitchen and a bathroom with a shower.

Now they were eating, the dad sitting in the camp chair and the two boys on the ground, holding their tin plates in their laps. What a simple life they had. When it came right down to it, you didn't really need a whole lot to survive—just food and water, shelter, and a latrine. Maybe everything they owned was right there at that campsite and in the camper of their pickup. A lot of people would feel sorry for them for that, but in some ways I thought they were lucky.

I sort of envied them, camping out up here in the high country. My family has never camped out, which is weird, considering our whole business is for people who want to get away from it all. I've noticed how people who come up from Phoenix always talk about how great our cabins are and how it helps them relax and think about what really matters in life.

I remember once handing the keys of a cabin over to a middle-aged guy who'd had this goofy grin on his face the whole time I was showing him where things were. He was so thrilled with how simple the cabins were. "Perfect! Nothing but the basics. A bed, a kitchen, a bathroom—what else do you need? I could live up here forever!"

But there wasn't anything more basic than a tent, a Coleman stove, and a hole dug for a latrine. Talk about the bare necessities.

Suddenly I felt guilty. Who was I to watch them through binoculars and decide if there was something wrong with the way their dad was raising them? I *hated* it when people looked at my parents and judged them.

It had happened more than once too. One time a couple of years ago, a woman who'd come into the store made a remark about how young the three of us were to be working. *How many hours do you work? Do you work every day? I hope you get time to play outside and just be kids.* The disapproval in her voice had put all five of us on edge.

"I like to work," Shea had piped up. She was only about eight at the time. Mom had clamped her jaw shut and kept quiet, but Rick had smiled at the lady through gritted teeth.

"Oh, don't worry," he'd told her. "They get lots of fresh mountain air up here. They're good kids. Now come back and see us again next time." He'd never say anything to insult the tourists.

Plus there was the fact that on rare occasions, like last week, Mom and Rick sometimes had to leave the three of us in charge of the store. They didn't like to do it, but if we weren't there to pitch in, they'd have to close up during those times.

And then there was Dad and his exceptional cooking skills. We eat out for practically every meal when we're visiting him, something that one of his neighbors sure noticed. She'd laughed when she saw us getting out of the car with bags from Taco Bell.

"Let's see, Brian. It was Denny's for breakfast, Taco Bell for lunch. You're going to poison them with all that fast food garbage. Where are you taking those poor kids for dinner tonight? KFC or Long John Silver's?"

"Nah, we're going high-class tonight—Olive Garden," Dad had answered her with a wink. But I'd felt like stuffing my burrito up her nose.

Hide and Seek

I wanted to go back to the cache site, to sneak away so that Jack and Sam wouldn't know I'd been watching them, but I was afraid that I might make a noise or do something that would attract their attention. So I stayed put, lying in the brushy undergrowth of the trees. I lowered the binoculars. Now it seemed like an invasion of their privacy to watch them. And I knew how they felt about snoops.

Chapter 10

After about ten or fifteen minutes, I noticed that they'd all gone into the tent, which gave me a chance to slip away and go back to where Dexter was waiting for me. He looked up and wagged his tail when he saw me coming, but he didn't even bother to stand up. He was pretty content lying in the shade and chewing his rawhide.

"You're being such a good dog!" I took his plastic bowl out of my backpack and gave him a drink. Then I unhooked his leash, and he shook his head and scratched.

I stretched out in the grass beside him and covered my eyes with my cap to shade them from the sun. The two of us waited there for another thirty minutes or so until Dexter stood up and wagged his tail when he saw Jack and Sam approaching. He knew them now, so he didn't need to bark at them.

When Sam saw me he ran up to me. "Did you bring candy?" He bounced up and down on his heels.

"You bet I did. And the surprise." I grinned at him. I was actually really happy to see these little guys.

"What's the surprise?" he asked, squirming in anticipation. Today he was wearing both of the oversized flip-flops. At least they matched.

"Well, we'll get to that in a minute. First, let's see what I brought." I unzipped my backpack and pulled out a towel to spread on the ground. Then I laid out the foil-wrapped pizzas, the bag of pineapple raisin muffins, and the stainless-steel water bottles. "We can have a picnic," I told the guys.

"Where's the candy?" asked Sam, his brow furrowing with a worried look.

"In here." I let him peek in my backpack to see, but I didn't take it out yet. "First things first, though. You can't eat the candy before you eat the real food, right?"

Jack nodded and poked Sam with his elbow.

"You guys hungry?" I asked, not letting on that I knew they just ate. They both nodded. I guess all kids can make room for pizza, even after a meal. I unwrapped the mini pizzas from the foil and handed one to each of them.

"You really did bring pizza!" Sam exclaimed.

"Sure, I told you I would."

It seemed weird to think that I'd only met them yesterday. Already it felt like the three of us were buddies. We sat in the grass and ate. I gave them one water bottle to share, and I poured water out for Dexter from my water bottle. Then I passed around the bag of muffins.

"These are my favorite. My mom makes them," I said.

Sam took a muffin from the bag and passed it to Jack. "My mom's dead."

I wasn't expecting such a blunt comment like that, just out of the blue. I swallowed a bite of muffin and cleared my throat. "Really? I'm sorry to hear that."

Jack stared at the ground and chewed and chewed. He wouldn't look at either of us. I felt so sorry for them. That must have been really tough for them to not have a mother, especially when they were both so young. And these poor little guys could really use some mothering. I wished that they could come home with me, even for a little while. My mom would feed them a big home-cooked meal and put them in clean clothes and read them a story. Every kid needed some of that.

"Yeah, but our dad's not dead. And we're not dead. And you're not dead," said Sam. "And Dexter's not dead!" He offered Dexter a piece of his pizza crust, and Dexter took it carefully in his teeth. He was really good at not biting the hand that was feeding him.

"Okay, now that we've eaten, we can have some candy." I pulled out a bag of M&M's, a package of Starburst, and some sour gummy worms. Sam practically climbed into my lap when he saw all the treats.

"Oh, I've had these before!" He grabbed the Starburst packet and ripped the wrapper open. "I love these!"

"Don't be so greedy," Jack told him. Sam had already stuffed three of the squares into his mouth and was chewing them into a big, gooey, multiflavored mass. Maybe I overdid it a little by bringing so much. It would be hard to keep them from eating all this candy at once.

Jack waited patiently until I offered him a sour worm. Then I opened up the M&M's and poured them out on the spread-out towel. "Let's split them up," I suggested. "Greens first. One for you, one for you, one for me."

The boys watched as I counted out all the M&M's by color. "This is the way my sisters and I always ate our M&M's when we were younger," I told them.

Jack nodded. "So it's even."

After we'd polished off all the candy and had a drink of water, I took the metal tackle box out of my backpack. "Now it's time for the surprise. Want to know what's in here?"

Hide and Seek

They both scooted closer and I could feel their warm breath on me, like a couple of puppies. I was used to having a little kid climb all over me because of Shea, but this was pretty cool, almost like having two little brothers. I didn't even mind their cheesy smell so much.

I opened up the box and showed them what was inside.

"Toys! Cool!" Sam shouted.

There were two miniature die-cast Tonka trucks—a dump truck and a backhoe—two glow-in-the-dark bouncy balls, some plastic dinosaurs, and four *Star Wars* action figures. I'd raided the plastic bin in Shea's room that was full of all these junky little toys. I knew Shea wouldn't miss these old toys; they were all mine to begin with anyway. I'd made a point of picking items that had at least two of everything, one for Jack and one for Sam.

When I'd first promised I'd bring surprises, I had no idea what they would be. My first thought was to just bring them some other snack I hadn't promised, like cookies or something. But I kept picturing Sam playing with his little army man in the dirt, so I came up with what I thought was a better idea.

Sam leaned against me, picking up the toys one by one and inspecting them. "Who's this guy?" he asked, holding up an action figure in an orange jumpsuit.

"That's a rebel fighter pilot. From *Star Wars*."

"Is it okay to play with these?" asked Sam.

"Of course. And you know what else? You can keep them."

They both looked surprised by that. I could tell Jack was thinking this over. "Maybe we better not." He was definitely the cautious one of the two.

"No, it's okay. I was thinking you could play with them now, and then we could find a good hiding place for this box. Kind of like a geocache of your own."

Sam gasped and his eyes widened. "Great idea!"

Jack did his little half-shrug. "Okay, I guess."

Pretty soon they had all the toys out of the tackle box and were busy playing with them in the grass. The Tonka trucks were the biggest hits. I cupped one of the bouncy balls in my hand and let them peek through my thumbs to see how they glowed in the dark.

They were both so happy with their new loot. It was fun watching them; I got the feeling they hadn't played with toys in a long time. Dexter napped in the grass nearby.

After playing around for a while, Sam started packing everything up and putting the toys in the box. "Let's hide it now, okay?"

"Sure. You guys look around and find a good spot."

Sam looked at me. "But what if somebody finds it and steals it?"

"Make sure you hide it really well. That's the fun of geo-caching—to hide a container so that only other geocachers will ever be able to find it. One time my uncle and I were looking for a geocache and we never found it, even with directions and clues."

"You think geocachers will find this?" asked Jack, clutching the box in his hands.

"Oh no, course not. Because we won't put the location on the website. No one but you guys will ever know it's there."

They both seemed satisfied with that answer, so they started looking around for a spot where they could hide it. At first Sam wanted to put the tackle box in the fallen log along with the ammo box, but Jack pointed out that a geocacher might find both containers.

"That's true," I agreed. "You'll want to hide it far enough

away from the real geocache so that anyone looking for it won't accidentally find yours," I told them.

So they kept looking. I held back and watched; I wanted this to be their own game of hide-and-seek.

"Let's bury it," Sam suggested.

"We don't have anything to dig with," Jack pointed out.

"We've got a shovel in the truck," Sam reminded him.

"No, we can't wake up Dad," Jack whispered.

Then Jack came up with a great location. He was crawling over some big boulders and found a spot among them where the box fit just right. The only problem was that if anyone else climbed around on the boulders, they'd spot the metal box hidden between the rocks. Not that I thought that was very likely, but the idea was to hide the container completely.

"Maybe you can find some dead leaves or something to cover it up so no one can see it," I suggested.

They both looked around and Sam picked up a rock. "Let's put this on top."

"Good idea," I said. Sam's rock mostly covered it, but looking down between the boulders, you could still see one corner of the tackle box.

"It needs another rock," said Jack, scrambling over the boulders to find something suitable. When he came back, he and Sam repositioned the two smaller rocks so that the tackle box was completely covered. If anyone happened to be exploring here, they'd have to go to the trouble of picking up all the rocks.

"Great job, guys!" I gave them both high fives. "You two are natural-born treasure hiders. Now any time you want to play with these toys, you can come take them out of your hiding spot."

Sam reached up and grabbed my Suns cap. Then he put it on his own head and grinned at me. "I stole your hat," he said proudly.

"I can see that," I said. It was a purple hat with the orange Suns logo of a flaming basketball on it. "You like the Suns?" I pushed the bill down to cover his eyes.

"No," said Sam. "I like the Packers." He repositioned the cap on his head so he could see.

"The Packers? Nobody likes the Packers!" I teased. "Anyway, that's football, you little goof. I'm talking about the NBA. If you're gonna wear my hat, you have to say you're a Suns fan."

"Okay. I'm a Suns fan."

Jack yanked my cap off of Sam's head and put it on his own. "I'm a Suns fan too."

By now it was after five o'clock, and I really needed to leave.

"Hey guys, I should probably go home now," I said.

"No!" said Sam. "Stay here!"

"I wish I could, but my parents are expecting me. They'll be worried if I don't show up soon."

"Are you coming back?" asked Jack, handing me my cap.

"I'll try. But tomorrow's Monday. I'll be in school all day. If I come, it'll have to be pretty late in the afternoon. Will you guys be able to come see me then?"

Jack shrugged. "Maybe."

"When's 'late afternoon'?" asked Sam.

"The earliest I could get here would be around four o'clock," I said. I wished they had some way to tell time. "Does your dad have a watch?"

Jack nodded. "Yeah, but…"

I realized they couldn't ask him what time it was without

making him suspicious. I looked down at my own watch. "Hey, I got an idea. I'll let you borrow mine." I took it off and showed it to Jack. "See? It's digital. Right now it says 5:26. When I come tomorrow, a four will be the first number. I can't promise I'll be here right at four-zero-zero, but it'll be somewhere around that time."

"I can tell time, even with a real clock," Jack said. "My mom taught me."

"I can't tell time," Sam admitted.

"You don't have to wear it on your wrist. You can keep it in your pocket," I said, knowing that he'd need to keep it out of sight around his dad.

Jack tucked the watch away. "But how are *you* gonna know the time?"

What a sharp little kid he was. I admired that. "Well, my GPS can tell me the time," I told him. I took it out of my backpack and showed it to them. "You guys ever seen one of these?" I asked.

They both shook their heads.

"Well, it's really cool. People use them to help find their way. It can show you maps and keep you from getting lost. A lot of people have them in their cars. GPS stands for Global Positioning System."

I turned it on, letting them watch the opening graphic, which was a picture of the earth and some orbiting satellites.

"See? It says, 'Wait...Tracking satellites.'" I pointed up to the sky. "It's finding satellites in space right now." We waited for a few seconds, watching the screen. "Now it says 'Ready to navigate.' See those little numbered dots? Those are the satellites it found."

They both stared at the screen while I talked. "See, there are lots of satellites orbiting around the earth, going around and around in circles all the time and sending back pictures and all kinds of information from space. A GPS is a receiver, and it picks up a signal that the satellite sends out."

I looked up at the sky and so did they. "You can't see them, but they're up there. They look kind of like spaceships, but there's nobody in them. The satellite sends information back that tells you 'This is the spot you're at right now.' See all those numbers? That's actually our latitude and longitude." I pointed to the bottom of the satellite screen where it showed our location.

"Then if there's another place you're trying to find, the satellite will help you navigate from where you are to where you're going. It can show you a map of your surroundings or point you in the right direction. The military first came up with these to help soldiers navigate when they were out in the field."

I showed them all the different display screens. "Now watch this." I selected the waypoint I'd marked for the ammo-box geocache and then showed them the navigation page. "It looks like a compass. See how the arrow swings around and points out the direction of the thing you're looking for?" They nodded and I let Jack hold the GPS.

"This is how I found the geocache in the first place. Someone had marked its location on a website, and I put that information into my GPS. Then I just had to follow the arrow and it took me right to it."

Jack held out the GPS and we walked around in circles. "Right now, it says we're 63 feet away from the log, and the arrow is pointing west. Watch how the number drops as we get closer." We walked slowly toward the log with the arrow pointing straight ahead and the number dropping with every step—63 feet, 57 feet, 42 feet. "Pretty cool, huh?"

"Can I see it?" asked Sam. I let him play around with the buttons for a while. But now it was really getting late, and I needed to go.

"Okay, so we have a plan?" I asked them, slipping the GPS back into the pocket of my cargo shorts. "I'll try to come tomorrow after school, sometime around four o'clock. You guys check the time and meet me here."

"Are you going to bring more candy?" asked Sam.

"Well, maybe a little candy, but if you eat as much as you ate today, I'd better bring along a dentist too." I poked him in the belly with my finger, and that made him laugh. "How about hot dogs tomorrow?"

"We love hot dogs!" Sam shouted, and Jack told him to quiet down.

"Okay, then. I'll see you tomorrow."

Chapter 11

That night at dinner, Rick told us something that almost made me choke. A short, red-haired guy came into the store right after I'd left and bought a bag of ice, a pack of cigarettes, and some canned beans.

"I didn't think that much about it till he left and I noticed that some fishing lures and two cans of lighter fluid were missing too. He was wearing a fishing vest with big pockets. Buy some merchandise, and then just help yourself to some more." Rick shook his head in disgust. "I'll never understand how people can do that."

A little surprised grunt escaped my throat before I could stop it. Rick looked up at me. "What's wrong with you?"

I closed my mouth which had been hanging open from shock. "Uh, nothing. I just wish I'd been there with you when it happened." I was glad the rest of them couldn't hear the way my heart had started to pound.

Mom frowned. "How did he pay?"

"With cash, of course. So there's no way to track him down."

"Was he by himself?" I asked, carefully cutting my chicken breast into bite sizes. "What kind of car was he driving?"

Rick shook his head. "I didn't really notice. A truck, I think. And yeah, he was alone."

Or at least alone in the store. Jack and Sam were probably waiting in the truck for him. It made me feel weird to think how close I'd come to running into all three of them on my own turf. Did they know their dad had gone into the store to buy a few things and steal some other stuff?

I could spill everything right now, tell the whole family that I knew who the shoplifter was, that he was camping out in the woods near Sheep's Crossing with his kids. But I didn't.

Rick would probably want to jump right in the car and drive out there to confront the guy. He wouldn't report him for shoplifting or anything; he'd just chew the guy out for stealing from him and demand the stuff back. But then how would Sam and Jack's dad catch fish or light a fire to feed his kids?

Shea sighed dramatically. "Another customer with sticky fingers." She sounded just like Mom saying that.

It wasn't the first time a customer had stolen from us, and it wouldn't be the last. It was just part of the business. We didn't have a lot of theft, but anytime you run a store, there's always a certain amount. Still, this was the first time I'd actually known who the thief was.

"Maybe he just couldn't afford to pay for everything. You know—he could just be somebody going through some hard times," I suggested.

Rick stopped chewing and frowned at me. "Fishing lures and lighter fluid aren't going to fill up an empty belly. Remember this, Chase. Anyone who walks out of the store without paying for our merchandise is stealing food right off this table." He pointed his fork at the meal spread out in front of us.

He was right. It did hurt us. It *was* like stealing money from my family. But it seemed like maybe our family could afford it better than theirs could right now. I wished I'd never even heard this conversation because now I felt bad for not telling them.

In the past I'd always had various reactions to shoplifters, from really mad to just annoyed. But it always surprised me that people could steal without feeling really guilty. I know I'd feel horrible taking stuff that didn't belong to me.

Lots of times it would be kids stealing candy or souvenirs without their parents noticing. That didn't bother me as much, but it sure drove Shea crazy because *she* knew stealing was wrong. Sometimes people seemed to do it just for the challenge, to see if they could walk out with something without getting caught. They never once stopped to think about how it hurt our family financially. Or maybe they just didn't care.

But this was the first time I'd ever thought that maybe sometimes people stole because they had to—because they really, really needed those items. Maybe it was easier to pay for the canned goods since they were harder to hide than fishing lures. If someone needed all of it but could only afford some of it, I could see how they might get desperate. I tried to picture Jack and Sam's dad again. Did he look desperate when I'd watched him this morning?

I thought again about how our cabins just sat empty in between guests. If that family really was homeless, maybe we could help them out. Couldn't they stay in one of our cabins, at least temporarily? Maybe the dad could get some extra money doing odd jobs around town. But would Mom and Rick ever go for something like that? The cabins were empty most of the time now, but if we had a good ski season this winter they wouldn't want to turn guests away.

After we'd cleared our plates and loaded the dishwasher, we all moved into the living room. Mom took the remote out of Kendra's hand and turned the TV off. Kendra hated family time on Sunday nights.

"Let's not have any distractions, okay?"

"Fine," said Kendra, slumping deep into the couch cushions. She'd rather be talking to her boyfriend Dave right now.

"Well, that lady who came over yesterday was the real estate agent," Rick started off.

"We're moving," said Shea flatly. She grabbed a throw pillow off the couch and squeezed it like a teddy bear.

"Now hold on a second. Let's talk about this," said Mom.

Why? Why did we have to keep talking about it? I just wished they wouldn't say anything else about moving until something was definite. I kept quiet and got busy laying the fire. I had the logs in place and was ready to add kindling. I pulled the stack of mail off the side table and started sorting through it for junk and flyers I could use.

Rick cleared his throat. "You all know that the past couple of winters have really hurt us. Not enough snow and not enough people coming up here during our second-busiest season." He paused for a second and scratched his beard thoughtfully. "This business would be great for your mom and me if you kids were already out of the house and we were close to retirement. That's who I suggested to the agent as the ideal buyer—an older couple, maybe. But someone who's still active enough to run the cabins and the store."

"But why can't it be a great business for a family with kids?" I wanted to know.

Mom sighed. "We've been able to get by and make a living. But we're not exactly rolling in dough, in case you haven't noticed." She nodded at the living room around us like she wanted us to note the complete absence of large quantities of cash lying around.

"I hate to admit it, but we haven't been able to save much of anything for college, and…" Mom's voice actually cracked a little, "and I lie awake at night wondering how we're going to be able to afford it."

"Dad will help," said Kendra.

"But we plan on doing our share too," said Rick. It kind of bothered him when Dad offered to pay for stuff for us that his child support didn't cover.

"That's right. We can't expect your dad to pay for everything," Mom agreed.

Around that point, I completely lost track of the conversation because I was staring at something that had caught my eye.

It was a white flyer, about the size of a letter. I'd seen hundreds of these in the mail. But for the first time ever, I really looked at it.

Have you seen us? the caption asked. Below it were two pictures, one of a young girl and the other of a woman who was probably her mother. Under their pictures were their names, dates of birth, and physical descriptions. Date missing: 11/20/2005. An 800 number and a website were also listed. I flipped the card over, and on the back was an ad for a dentist's office in Show Low.

Instead of tossing it into the fire with the rest of the junk mail, I slipped the flyer underneath the stack of bills and other important mail.

What if?

But they were with their dad. I was *sure* that man was their dad. All three of them looked exactly alike.

At least I thought they did. I'd never actually seen the guy up close. And why would the guy keep a lookout? Why were the kids so secretive?

Was there any chance that they could be—?

What if the dad—?

I took the poker and shifted the top log a little so it would catch better on one side. I stared into the flames with my back to everyone else. The heat of the fire warmed my face, and their voices sounded like some distant conversation on TV.

"Of course you have a say, but ultimately Rick and I will decide what we think is in your best interest," Mom was telling Kendra.

"It sure doesn't sound like you're considering how we feel at all," Kendra answered.

"This isn't an easy decision, alright?" Mom said. "Rick and I have thought about how tough a move would be on all of you."

Rick slapped his thighs like he'd just made up his mind. "Here's the deal. If we can find a buyer, we won't move till the end of the year, so that's a few months away. If we can't find a buyer...well, we'll stay here and keep running the store and the cabins." Rick paused and looked at all of us. "But I have to say that I'm hoping we find a buyer."

"Then why are we even discussing this? You guys made your executive decision and it's done," said Kendra.

Their voices droned on and on. I was getting really bored with this. I interrupted Mom in the middle of some big speech about the advantages of living in Phoenix. "I've got homework to do. Can I go up to my room now?" I stood up and started toward the staircase.

"Wait a second," she said without even looking at me.

I sat back down and shoved a rolled-up piece of newspaper

between two burning logs just to watch it burst into flames. What good did it do to discuss everything to death?

"You totally control our lives right now," said Kendra. "If you decided we should drop out of society and go live in a commune with some crazy guy who thinks he's God's second cousin, we'd have to do it."

Shea giggled over that, and I almost laughed too. But then I thought of Jack and Sam again. They weren't living in a commune, but it did look like they'd dropped out of society.

"There's always a chance we'll put everything up for sale and we won't find a buyer." Mom sounded completely exhausted.

"That's true," Rick agreed. "We just thought it was time to let you guys know what's going on. We figured you were mature enough to take part in this discussion." He raised his eyebrows at Kendra. "Obviously, we were very wrong about the mature part."

Kendra snatched away Shea's throw pillow and tossed it at Rick. "Don't call me immature!" she wailed in a little-girl voice. She'd definitely benefit from some courses in drama school.

"Don't make me spill my beer!" Rick yelled with a laugh and tossed the pillow back at her. At least now everyone was laughing, which was far more normal than this serious discussion we'd been having.

I blew on the tiny flames I had going in the fireplace. My life might change pretty radically in the next year. But that was something I didn't want to think about.

Chapter 12

Three hot dogs? You're eating *three* hot dogs?" Kendra asked me when we got home from school Monday afternoon. I was standing in front of the microwave, waiting for them to heat up.

"Two for me, one for Dexter," I said, taking them out and sticking them into buns. I like mustard, but I didn't bother with it today because I was in a hurry. I yanked off a piece of foil and wrapped them up.

"That dog does not need a hot dog," Kendra told me.

"Oh, yeah? Try telling him that." I grabbed my outdoor backpack from the counter and stuffed the hot dogs inside.

Shea followed me out the door. "Where are you going? Every day you take off somewhere and you're gone for hours."

"No place," I said. "I'm just going for a bike ride."

She ran to catch up with me. "Every single day? Are you riding over to Carly Hudson's house?" she asked, and I almost walked smack into the side of the shed.

"No! What are you talking about?" I yelled at her. My face got hot. What did she know about Carly Hudson? I ducked into the shed and pulled my bike out.

"Well, she likes Joseph Hernandez anyway," Shea said, coming right in behind me. "But I know you're up to something. If you weren't, you'd let me go along."

"Look, if you'll stop pestering me, I'll go for a bike ride with you when I get back, alright? See you later." *Joseph Hernandez.* Why'd she have to mention that dork's name?

I hopped on my bike and was down the road before Dexter even caught on to what was up. He raced after me. Why was it such a big deal for me to have time to myself? I made a growling sound in my throat and Dexter's ears perked up.

"Shea had better keep her mouth shut," I told him. I didn't like the idea of her being so suspicious. I glanced over my shoulder to make sure the little spy wasn't following me. Didn't she have a store to run?

When I got close to our meeting place, I could see Jack and Sam already waiting for me.

"You're late!" said Sam. I noticed they had the tackle box in front of them with some of the toys out.

I skidded to a stop and climbed off my bike. "Give me a break," I told him, pulling out my GPS to check the time. "It's only 4:03. That's as close to being on time as I could get."

"Well, we've been waiting since 3:51," Sam announced. "And that's a really long time." He held up my watch and waggled it in front of me.

"We can't stay long," said Jack, looking over his shoulder. "Dad might be waking up soon."

"Okay, no problem. I can't stay long today either," I told them. "But at least we have time for a snack."

I pulled out the foil package and opened it up. "Just like I promised. Hot dogs." They each took one and I split mine with Dexter. He ate his half in two bites, his tail wagging the whole time.

Hide and Seek

We sat in the grass to eat and enjoy the nice fall weather. The aspens were really starting to turn now. The whole mountainside was sprinkled with gold and yellow and orange.

"These are yummy," said Sam with his mouth full. "We used to eat these a long time ago."

"I thought you had a stomachache," Jack said to him.

"I did, but it feels better now," said Sam. "These hot dogs help."

Jack glanced at me and cleared his throat. "We might be leaving soon," he said.

I looked at them both. "Really? Going home?" I asked.

They gave each other the brother look. "Not yet. We'll just move to a new spot," said Jack.

"We move around a lot," said Sam. "And we've been here for a long time now."

"Do you know where you're going?" I asked.

Jack shrugged. "I'm not sure. It might be someplace close by or we might be moving on."

"Yeah, moving on is when we pack up and take a long, long, *long* car ride," said Sam. He chewed another bite of hot dog and let out a sigh. "Then I guess it'll be time to change the plate."

"Change what plate?" I asked him.

"Don't you know about changing the plate?" asked Sam. "Whenever you go into a new state, you have to change the plate. Dad takes off the old one and gets rid of it. Then he puts on a new one."

I was about to explain to them that you only had to do that if you were moving permanently to a new state, that it was fine to have out-of-state tags if you were only driving through. But something about their story sounded a little strange.

"Oh, you mean the *license* plate. On the car," I said. "I've always lived in Arizona, so I don't know that much about changing plates. So, what do you do? Go to an office and buy a new plate?" I suggested.

Jack and Sam both shook their heads.

"Nope. You just get a new one. You have to go out and find one." Jack looked up and squinted. "Texas...New Mexico... Utah. Those are the ones I can remember. We've had lots."

Alarm bells started ringing inside my brain. I could feel my pulse throbbing in my neck, but I tried to keep my expression exactly the same as it was.

"Are you sure you don't have to go to an office to do this?" I asked. "Where do the new ones come from?"

Jack shrugged. "Dad just gets them. He puts the new one on with a screwdriver and throws the old one away. That way the cops won't hassle us. If you're driving in a state with the wrong plate, the cops might pull you over and hassle you," he explained.

"Yeah, cops are snoopy," Sam agreed. "They can arrest you and throw you in jail for no reason. And they take kids away from their parents. You can't trust cops."

I nodded slowly. Now sirens were going off, screaming out a deafening blare that only I could hear. Dexter sat in his sphinx pose with his paws out in front of him, blinking and panting with a look of absolute contentment on his face. But I was trying not to shiver in the warm afternoon sunlight.

"Why would they take kids away from their parents?" I managed to ask finally.

"Because they're *bad* guys," said Sam, acting like I didn't have a clue. "They don't even need a reason." He pointed his finger at me. "Never, never, never talk to the cops," he warned.

He said it in his cute little kid voice, but it still turned the blood in my veins to ice water.

I wiped my mouth with the back of my hand and tried to think of what to say next. "I thought cops were supposed to *obey* the laws and keep everybody else from breaking them. And don't they help people if they get in trouble?" I asked. "If there's an emergency, aren't you supposed to call 911 so a cop can come help you?"

"Don't ever trust a cop," Jack said knowingly. "They're all crooked."

I felt like leaning over and barfing up my hot dog in the grass beside me. What kind of garbage was their dad telling them?

I looked at their dirty little faces. They were such little kids; Jack was probably Shea's age, and Sam was even younger than that. What kinds of things had they gone through already in their short lives? Their mother dying, moving all over with their dad who was a shoplifter and a...I didn't even know the word for someone who stole license plates off cars. Was he wanted or something? A criminal on the run with his kids along?

I took a long, deep breath. "Are you sure you're going to be leaving soon?" I asked, remembering how this whole horrible conversation had started. A cool breeze blew past, fluttering the aspen leaves and drying the sweat that had broken out on my forehead.

"Maybe," said Jack. "Dad said it was about time to find a new campsite. That's how we do it."

Sam gazed into the tackle box. "I wish we could take our toys with us." He looked up at me. "They're ours to keep, right?"

"Right. You could take some of them in your pockets, maybe. So your dad wouldn't see them."

Sam sorted through the contents of the tackle box. "But not the dinosaurs. They're too pokey." He ran his finger along the plastic horns of a triceratops.

"I wish you guys knew when you were leaving. And where you're going. Are you sure your dad didn't mention the name of a campground or a lake or something?" I was trying to come up with something—anything. If they could just give me the name of someplace close by that I recognized…

Jack shook his head. "He didn't say. All he said was we'd be leaving here pretty soon."

"I'm going to miss you guys. We're starting to be buddies," I said, because it was true. Would they get enough to eat? Would they ever go to school? What was going to happen to them?

Sam stared at the ground in front of him and I could see his chin puckering up like he was about to cry. I took my Suns cap off and put it on his head, pulling the bill down low to hide his face.

"Hey, cut it out!" he said with a laugh, and I was glad I'd changed his mood. I felt like giving them my phone number or my address so they could get in touch with me later, but I realized that was ridiculous.

It bothered me that their dad was involved in some criminal activity. It was one thing for him to shoplift food if his family was hungry, but stealing license plates was completely different.

If only I could sneak them away from here and hide them out in one of our cabins. I could bring them food, keep them safe. If I thought I could convince them to come with me, I just might do it.

Hide and Seek

Maybe I should tell Mom and Rick. Just start at the beginning and tell them everything—tell them about how suspicious this all seemed. Something wasn't right. I just knew it.

But would they believe me? Or would they think it was none of our business? If they did think something was wrong and we should get involved, what would they do?

Now Jack was looking at me. "So we might be here tomorrow. But"—his shoulder hitched up—"we might not."

I thought about this for a second. "I could try to find you, if you move to a new campsite nearby."

It was a crazy thing to say, and it was probably a bad idea for me to get their hopes up, but I said it anyway. Because I was hoping I could somehow find them again. I felt like they needed me.

"But how? We don't know where we're going," said Jack.

"I know. That's what makes it tough," I admitted. I started having all kinds of crazy thoughts, like running home and grabbing some walkie-talkies to give them. I glanced at Dexter. I wished I could tell him to follow their trail so we could find them again.

"Let's think about this for a second," I said, and they both cupped their chins in their hands and propped their elbows on their knees like I was doing.

A trail. If only there was some way they could leave a trail. "Hold on a second," I said. "Let's look at our supplies and see if we can come up with any ideas."

I emptied my backpack and spread my stuff out in the grass. Binoculars, my GPS plus some extra AAs for it, water bottles, the flashlight I'd put in after that evening Dexter took off on me, a Swiss Army knife, Dexter's water bowl, leash, and the duck call I'd taken out of the geocache on the first day.

Sam immediately picked up my binoculars and started

looking through them. Then he grabbed the duck call. "What's this thing?" he asked, turning it over.

"Blow right there and it makes a funny sound," I told him. He did, and Dexter reacted the same way he had on the first day: ears up and a startled look on his face. Sam and Jack both cracked up over that. Sam was about to blow it again when Jack stopped him. "Better not. What if Dad hears it?"

While they were looking through my stuff, I had another idea. I ran over to the log, pulled out the ammo box, and brought it over to where we were sitting. "Let's look in here too," I said, opening the latches and emptying out all the contents.

Besides the log book, there were rubber snakes, the red bandana and bottle opener I'd left, a padlock and key, Allen wrenches, two army men, a die-cast Jeep, two strands of plastic beads, and the wooden nickel.

"What are we doing?" asked Sam, squatting in the dirt next to me and breathing his warm breath on my arm.

"Trying to think of something," I said, staring at the contents of my backpack and the geocache. "The duck call is excellent. We can definitely use that."

What about my Swiss Army knife? Should I give it to Jack and tell him to carve some kind of marks on nearby trees for me to try to find?

That wasn't such a good idea.

But...maybe...

"Okay," I announced. "I have a plan."

Chapter 13

I'm not sure this will work, but we can try it. If you guys happen to move to a new campground that's somewhere around here, maybe I can find you again on my bike. I'm giving you these things to take with you." I gathered Dexter's leash, the strings of beads, and the duck call into a pile.

The three of us crouched in the dirt and I explained my idea. "Wherever you camp, there has to be a road nearby for the truck. If I could find that road, I might be able to find where your campground is—if you leave me a few markers."

I handed Jack the leash. "Here's what I want you to do. After your dad has set up your new camp, pay attention to where the nearest road is. Then when you get a chance, go back to it and tie Dexter's leash around a tree trunk. Tie it up high enough so that I can see it from the road. Like this."

I went over to a nearby aspen and wrapped Dexter's leash around it at a height of about four feet. Luckily, it was red nylon, so it was colorful enough to see from a distance. Jack and Sam came and stood by my elbow, watching me.

"See? This will be a marker to let me know your camp is close by," I explained, and Jack nodded solemnly.

Then I went over and picked up the strands of beads, one purple and one gold. "After you've tied the leash to a tree, you can drop these beads to leave a trail from the tree to your campsite. Hopefully, that will lead me to where you guys are." I was getting really excited. Plus I was feeling pretty proud of myself for coming up with this idea. I thought it was slightly ingenious.

"But how will we get 'em off?" asked Sam, taking the purple strand from me and examining it.

"Just break the necklace and pull them off like *this*." I held up the gold strand and yanked it with both hands, and the thread broke, but the beads didn't come sliding off. To get one off, I had to grab it and tug it. It snapped off the string.

"Here. Try it." I handed the broken strand to Jack and let him pull off a few beads.

"Let me have a turn too," Sam insisted.

"Okay, but don't pull them all off now because you might lose a few. Now, the last thing I'm going to have you guys take is the duck call." I held it up. "If you get a chance late in the afternoon, try sneaking away to somewhere close to the road and blowing it. If I happen to be out looking for you, I might be able to hear it. But don't bother unless it's late in the day, because you know I'll be in school until then."

Jack nodded and put the duck call in his pocket. Sam tucked the strands of beads into his pockets. I unwrapped Dexter's leash from the tree and handed it to Jack.

"Where should I put it?" he asked, since it was obviously too big to cram inside a pocket.

I wished they had jackets on, but they were wearing the same T-shirts I'd seen them in on Saturday. "Let's try hiding it under your shirt," I suggested, turning him around and stuffing the folded leash up the back of his shirt. I tucked the tail of his T-shirt into his jeans, but it still made a huge bulge.

I shook my head, feeling stupid that I hadn't thought

about that before. My great plan wasn't so great after all if I didn't have something for them to use as a marker.

"This isn't going to work," I admitted, pulling the leash out. "Your dad would definitely see that under your shirt. Unless you could somehow sneak it into your campsite and keep him from seeing it?" I asked.

Jack gazed at the leash and chewed on his bottom lip. "I don't know."

"We could tell him we found it," suggested Sam.

"He'd tell us to leave it," Jack said. "Or he'd take it away from us."

I glanced at the items spread out in the grass in front of us. "Wait a second. If Plan A fails, go to Plan B," I said, grabbing the red bandana. "Instead of the leash, let's use this!" I went back to the aspen and tried to tie the bandana around the trunk, but it wouldn't go all the way around, so I tied it to a low branch instead. Then I walked backwards and stood several feet away to see how it looked.

"It's a good alternative," I told the guys. "It's colorful. Remember to tie it as close to a nearby road as possible and high enough for me to see it."

Jack looked at the bandana and frowned. "Is this going to work?"

"I'm not sure," I admitted. "Pay attention to how long you're riding in the truck and try to notice your surroundings. If you're driving for a long time, say, over an hour, then don't even bother because you'll be too far away from here. But if it's just another campground near here...*maybe* I can find you."

"I hope so," said Sam.

I knelt in front of him. "Yeah, me too, buddy. But I can't make any promises. I'll do my best, okay?" I held out my hand for him to bump fists.

"Okay."

Jack had gone over to the tree to take the bandana off, and he was busy folding it into a neat square. "Can you see it?" he asked us, tucking it into his back jeans pocket.

"Nope. Can't see it at all," I assured him. "Now remember, the only time I can come for the next few days is late in the afternoon because of school. I'll check here first tomorrow, but if you're not here, I'll start riding around other camp-grounds and stuff to try to find you."

Jack nodded. I could tell he'd listened to all my instruc-tions and was trying to keep everything straight. "Here's your watch. You better take it back. In case...if you can't find us."

"Okay." I took it from him and put it on my wrist. Then we packed up all the items from the geocache and my back-pack. Since I'd taken a couple of items out of the cache, I left my extra AA batteries in the ammo box. Take something, leave something—that's the rule. Jack started putting the toys away in the tackle box.

"Can't we keep some of the toys in case we don't come back?" asked Sam.

"If you have room in your pockets," Jack answered. So Sam took out the rebel fighter pilot in the orange jumpsuit and tucked him deep into his jeans pocket.

Jack paused for a few seconds like he couldn't decide if he wanted to take anything or not, but then he reached in and picked out a battle droid from *The Clone Wars*. "I guess I'll take this one," he said with his little embarrassed shrug. He was always so serious compared to Sam.

"Let's hide the box anyway. In case we come back," Sam said, so we closed it up and took it back to their hiding spot among the boulders.

"We better go. If Dad wakes up and we're not close by, he gets kinda mad," said Jack.

I glanced at my watch. It was after five. "Yeah, I need to go too. But I'll come back tomorrow. And who knows, maybe you'll still be here."

Sam wouldn't look at me. Jack just stood there and nodded.

"Okay, high fives, guys." I held up my hand for them to slap. "See ya."

Then I hopped on my bike and took off with Dexter racing to get in front of me.

I didn't like long good-byes.

I figured they didn't either.

Chapter 14

All the way home, my head buzzed. All that crazy stuff about stealing license plates, and cops being bad guys. What was up with that? I'd always felt like something wasn't right about those kids, and now I was beginning to suspect things were seriously messed up.

As soon as I got home, Shea came right out.

"Did you have a good time on your *bike ride?*" she asked.

"Yeah, it was amazing," I told her. Did she really think I was riding over to Carly's house? If she ever tried to say one word to Carly on the bus, I might have to sit on her.

"You said we'd go for ride when you got back. Let's go!" She ran to get her bike out of the shed.

I was totally not in the mood for this, but I *had* promised her.

So we went on a short bike ride with my sister talking the whole time, and me feeling blown away by all this new information.

Maybe it was time for me to tell Mom and Rick about these strange little kids I'd met in the woods. All I'd have to say was that I knew where our shoplifter was, and Rick would want to see their campsite for himself.

Then what? Would he confront the guy? Or call the sheriff? The boys were scared to death of cops. I didn't want them traumatized.

"Shea, it's almost dark. We should go in now," I called to her. She was riding just ahead of me, barely visible in the dusk.

"Just a few minutes longer," she yelled over her shoulder. "I can still see."

"I'm getting cold. I'm going in now, but you can stay out if you want."

I knew that would get to her. She did a U-turn and came pedaling up to me. "Fine! But you're such a wimp sometimes, Chase."

"I know," I said.

Once we were inside, I headed straight to the side table in the living room, pulled out the flyer I'd left there last night and tucked it into the pocket of my cargo shorts. Then I went to the computer in the upstairs office. I wanted to close the door, but I figured that might look suspicious.

My fingers trembled as I slipped the flyer out of my pocket and typed the web address into the browser. It was a website for missing children, and when the home page popped up, I saw all these pictures of little kids staring at me. On the left, there was a toolbar with a link for people to report a sighting. My fingers hovered over the keyboard. I wasn't sure there'd been a sighting. I was too nervous to even click on the link to see where it would take me.

There was a *quick search* option to help find missing children, so I decided to start there. I checked the box marked *male* and used the dropdown menu to pick *Arizona*. That's one of the advantages of living in a state at the beginning of the alphabet; we never have to scroll down very far, unlike the people in Wyoming or Vermont.

In the *missing within __ years* box, I typed "four," which I figured gave me plenty of leeway. Five boys popped up. I was so relieved when none of them were Jack and Sam. Next I tried searching in the other states Jack had mentioned—Texas, Utah, and New Mexico. Still nothing. Another sigh of relief.

Then I clicked on *other search options*, which took me to a screen where I could enter all kinds of information: names, dates missing, physical description, and case type.

I took a deep breath and tried to fill in as much informa-tion as I could, starting with Jack. For *missing date*, I again put in "four years." For *missing from which state*, I selected *all*. I did the same for *possible location*. Now I was down to *physical description*. I entered his current age as "between eight and twelve," again trying to keep it really broad. Sex: *male*. Race: *white*. Hair color…wow, I couldn't believe all the choices. Was Jack's hair blonde, red, or sandy? It was somewhere in the range of all three of those. I went with blonde. Eye color? I couldn't remember.

Case type? There were all kinds of choices: endangered missing, endangered runaway, family abduction, non-family abduction, lost. I chose *all*. Then I hit Search.

No records found.

Okay. But if I changed some things around….

I spent probably twenty minutes doing various searches on Jack, John, Jackson, Sam, and Samuel. I tried them with sandy, red, and blonde hair from ages four to thirteen. I even changed their race to *all*. A couple of times I got pictures of kids who weren't Jack or Sam, but most of the searches came up *No records found.*

Whew. It was actually a huge relief not to find them on this website. If I *had* found them, I had no idea what my next step would have been. I clicked on the picture of one little girl. She was six when the picture was taken, but her age now was listed as ten. Her case type was "lost, injured, missing."

Unbelievable. Four years of her family not knowing where she was or what had happened to her. It looked like they'd used a school photo; her hair was perfectly curled and she had a purple ribbon that matched her purple dress. I clicked back to the home page because I couldn't stand looking at her any longer. She'd be just about Shea's age now.

On the home page, I let the cursor hover over the *Report a Sighting* link, but I didn't click on it. I exited out of the website. I was actually shivering when I stood up to leave the office.

It had gotten pretty cold in the house, but that wasn't the only reason I was shaking.

Chapter 15

On Tuesday afternoon, I rode my mountain bike right up to the spot where Jack and Sam's campsite had been. There was no need to be careful now. I could tell from a distance that no one was there. The patch of dirt among the trees was completely barren. No truck, no tent, no camp stove—nothing. Just some tire tracks in the dirt.

"It's not looking good, Dexter," I said out loud. "They must've left a while ago."

I got off my bike and squatted down to look at the tracks. If I were a detective trying to solve a case, I could take a mold of these tracks and figure out what brand of tires had left them. I wasn't sure how that information would help me, but that's what they did on TV.

There were a few footprints in the dirt—little ones and bigger ones that crisscrossed over each other. But other than that, there wasn't any sign that Jack and Sam and their dad had even been here.

Some detective I am, I thought. I hadn't even bothered to find out what make and model their white pickup was.

Dexter sniffed all around and marked a bunch of trees. Then he sniffed for so long at one spot in the grass that I got curious and walked over to see what he'd found. It was a puddle with a few cubes of ice melting in the middle. A strong smell of fish hit me when I bent down.

A real detective would be able to determine how long they'd been gone by how much ice was left in the puddle. He'd probably even know a formula: *A ten-pound bag of ice emptied on the ground will melt at a rate of __ hours when the outside temperature varies from __ to __ degrees.*

I wished I was a real detective. But I wasn't. Still, the ice wasn't completely melted, so I guessed they couldn't have been gone that long. Maybe they'd left last night, or this morning, or even a few hours ago. How cold had it been last night? Into the low forties, I thought. And today it was probably mid-sixties, and this spot was in the shade, under the trees. But I had no way of knowing how much ice was in the cooler to begin with and it...

Oh, what was the point? They were gone. That was all that really mattered.

I stood up and looked through the trees toward the road to Big Lake. Which way had they gone? If only Jack had drawn an arrow in the dirt, pointing out the direction they took.

Then I had a sudden idea. What if?

I picked up my bike and took off, bouncing over the bumpy ground and through the trees till I reached the log. I found the ammo box and took out the memo pad, my fingers fumbling to get to the last page. Maybe, just maybe, Jack had had a chance to leave me a message about where they were going.

But there was nothing new. I punched my thigh with my balled-up fist. Why hadn't I thought of this yesterday? I felt like kicking myself for not telling him to try to leave me a note.

"How are we ever going to find them?" I asked Dexter. Yesterday I'd been so hopeful, but now I was feeling totally discouraged. What were the odds that they'd just be moving to a new spot somewhere close by? And even if they did do that, how close could they possibly be? Ten miles away was no distance at all in a pickup truck, but it was a long trip for me to make on my bike, even if I knew where I was heading. How long would it take me to cover a ten-mile radius while I looked for a red bandana?

I thumbed through the memo pad and ripped out all the messages that the boys and I had written. Then I put everything back the way it was. I had a feeling I wouldn't be doing much with this geocache again.

Next I went over to the boulders where the boys had stashed their own private cache of toys. I moved the two small rocks, and found the tackle box right where we'd left it. I opened it up and checked the toys. Nothing new here. I decided to put the tackle box back in my backpack. Jack and Sam were gone now, so there wasn't any point in leaving it.

"Okay, Dext. Let's go." I climbed on my bike and we headed for the road. I had a heavy feeling in my chest. I couldn't figure out why I'd gotten so attached to those little guys so fast. I felt like they needed me in some way. I'd been ready to rescue them if they were lost, and when they turned out not to be lost—just hungry—I guess feeding them had been the next best thing. I really wondered if they'd be okay without me. Somehow I felt like their dad hadn't been taking very good care of them.

"Think we can find them?" I asked Dexter. He trotted along beside me with his mouth hanging open. Instead of going east down the hiking trail to Sheep's Crossing, back the way we always came, I headed toward the campsite again. When we got to the bare patch of dirt under the trees, I stared at the tire tracks in the dust. I could easily see the path the truck had taken north to get to the road. I slid my backpack off my shoulders, took out my GPS, and turned it on. Once it had picked up the signals, I went to the navigation page. Then I started following the tire tracks across the meadow. Dexter seemed excited that we were heading across new terrain.

By the time we reached the paved road, we'd gone .36 miles north from the campsite. Now the dusty tire tracks stopped, and I looked first one way down the paved road and then the other. Which way? I held my GPS up like it knew which way they'd gone, but it didn't tell me anything. If I went east down this road, it would take me back to the 373 and right into Greer—to my house, the store, and the cabins. But Big Lake was west, about thirty miles away. If that's where they were headed, I sure couldn't follow them on my bike.

I had to think about this logically. They'd been fishing on Sunday morning, and they'd stopped at the store to buy ice, cigarettes, and canned goods and to steal fishing lures and lighter fluid. That meant they must have been fishing at one of the nearby reservoirs. Sure, they could've gone all the way to Big Lake to fish, but in that case why wouldn't they have camped someplace near there? It just wasn't logical for them to camp here but then drive thirty miles to fish.

Maybe—possibly—their dad had decided to move their campsite closer to the reservoirs. It was worth a shot. I'd promised Jack and Sam that I would try to find them.

"This way, Dext," I called, turning east to go back into town. As I pedaled along, I perked up a little. I even started looking at the passing trees, checking for the red bandana. What if I was actually able to find them again? What if my tracking scheme really worked? That would be so cool!

When I didn't see any sign of the bandana by the time we got back to the 373, I tried not to let it bother me. I still had all the area around the reservoirs to search, and there were tons of ideal spots around there for camping.

We turned down the road that would take us to the reservoirs. The late afternoon sun came slanting through the trees, making a pattern of light and shade on the pavement in front of me. I slowed my bike to a gentle roll so I could scan the trees for a flash of red cloth. We had three reservoirs to explore—Bunch, River, and Tunnel. Any one of them could've been where Jack and Sam had gone trout fishing with their dad on Sunday.

Out of the corner of my eye, I caught a glimpse of movement, so I braked to a stop and looked up. There, about a hundred feet up the hill in among the ponderosa pines, I saw a pair of deer. They stood absolutely frozen, watching us to see what we would do. Dexter hadn't spotted them because they weren't moving and they were far enough away from us. So I kept still too and didn't make a sound.

It was a buck and a doe, and then a shadow moved behind the buck and I saw they had a fawn with them too. A whole family! I was dying to take out my binoculars for a closer look, but I was afraid that any movement I made might cause them to startle and run. So I just stood there, straddling my bike, my hands resting on the handlebars. I wanted to see how long I could watch them before they'd bolt up the hill through the trees.

The buck stared at me, unmoving. The trees between us obscured my view a little, but I could still see his strong brown body, the curved prongs of his antlers, and his shiny black eyes. His large ears turned in and out slightly as he tried to pick up all the noises around him.

Hide and Seek

The little fawn had gotten bored with watching me and was nibbling around in the grass. The doe was slowly moving up the hill, but she'd turn her graceful neck and stop to look at us every few feet.

I slowly let out my breath, realizing I'd been holding it in. The buck turned away and moved up the hill to follow his mate. The fawn took a few short hops behind its mother, who was picking her way up the hillside on her delicate legs.

It was so incredible to watch them. I felt a sudden rush of envy. What if I could switch places with them and live out here like they did in the woods? So peaceful, so content, so in tune with nature.

They reached the top of the hill and disappeared from my view, but I kept staring after them, wishing they'd come back. And what was I thinking? It was stupid to assume deer didn't have a care in the world. Of course they did. They had to find food and water; they had to look out for predators, both human and animal. Survival—that was their one objective. All day, every day. They didn't have an easy life at all.

I wondered suddenly, who had it easier? Me, or Jack and Sam? My first answer would've been to say that I had it easier. I'd never known real hunger, the kind that gnaws at your belly for days at a time when you just don't have enough food to put in it. I took hot showers, dressed in clean clothes, and slept in a warm bed every night with a roof over my head. I definitely had a more comfortable life.

But maybe a part of me envied Jack and Sam just a little. Their lives were so simple, so basic. They didn't have school and homework and chores. Their lives were certainly less complicated than mine, in lots of ways. They just lived one day at a time.

Were they happy with their lives? Would they switch places

with me if they had the chance? It seemed like at one time they'd had a more normal childhood—school, toys, pizza, and a mom who'd taught Jack to tell time. Now they moved around all over the place, living in a tent and eating fish they'd caught that day. It wasn't a comfortable life, but they were surviving. Would I…would I switch places with them?

I shook myself out of my trance and slid back onto the seat of my bike. The deer were long gone, and I still had a lot more ground to cover before darkness came.

Chapter 16

I didn't find them. I spent a couple of hours riding my bike around the reservoirs that afternoon, but I never saw a sign of a red bandana or a white pickup truck. It had been a long shot. I'd known that all along, but I just didn't want to admit it.

Wednesday afternoon, for the first time in a week, I didn't go back to the geocache site. There wasn't any point now. Instead, when I got home from school, I went straight upstairs to my room and stretched out on my bed. I had the whole house to myself, something that didn't happen too often. Shea had gone home with her friend Morgan, and Kendra had stayed after school with some friends to work on a research project. Mom was teaching her class, and Rick was at the store.

I'd told Rick I'd come by to help out when I got home, but I wanted a little time to myself first. A nice breeze was coming in through my open window, and part of me wished I could just lie here on my bed all afternoon and not do a thing— not work in the store, or watch TV, or do homework, or even ride my bike all over the place.

I needed some new project to work on. Something to take my mind off Jack and Sam. They'd be okay, wouldn't they?

Maybe they were heading toward Phoenix where it'd be nice and warm all winter.

What good did it do for me to sit here thinking about them, anyway? I should find something to do. Maybe it was time for me to put together my own geocache and hide it someplace. But I didn't really feel like doing that today.

What I *should* do was go by Jim Greenfield's house and ask when he wanted me to chop firewood with him. That's something I really needed to take care of. But I sure didn't feel like getting off my bed to go and do that.

I heard toenails clicking up the wooden staircase, and then Dexter walked in, his tail wagging expectantly and his ears pushed forward.

"What do you want?" I asked. He just wagged his tail and waited for me to get up. "I know. I'm being lazy today." I scratched his ear, hoping he'd leave me alone after that, but of course he didn't.

I rolled over and faced my window, turning my back to Dexter. I should've gone home with Chris today or asked him to come over here. I'd barely hung out with any of my friends since school had started.

I felt pressure on the edge of my mattress, so I rolled back over. Dexter was standing there with both of his front paws on the edge of my bed.

"They're gone, Dext. Jack and Sam left. If we go back there, the only thing we'll see is maybe a few elk." His tail wagged, and he pawed at me.

My Suns cap was hanging on my bedpost, so I grabbed it and put it on Dexter's head. "If you're gonna wear my cap, you gotta say you're a Suns fan," I told him. The bill hid his eyes from my view. "Or maybe you prefer the Packers."

The Packers?

Hide and Seek

The *Green Bay* Packers! I stopped dead still, my mouth slightly open, my hand hovering in midair. The cap slid off Dexter's head and fell to the floor. I didn't move or breathe or even blink. The Packers. Why would a kid from Arizona like the Packers?

Because they weren't from Arizona. Maybe…maybe they were from…

Suddenly the phone rang—a loud, shrill noise that made me jump and jolted my heart into beating again. I sprang off the bed and ran to the office down the hall.

"Hello?"

"Chase, what're you up to?" Rick said. "I thought you were coming in to keep me company."

I stood beside the desk, staring at the dark computer screen. "Uh, yeah. I kind of fell asleep." Well, not quite asleep, but I felt like I was in a dream.

"You fell asleep? What's wrong—you getting sick or something?"

"I don't know. Maybe. My throat's a little sore." I swallowed. My throat was fine. It was my head that was about to explode right now.

"Uh-oh. That doesn't sound good. Well, just stay home then. I can't afford to get sick too."

"Are you sure you don't need me?" I asked, regretting my lie. "I really don't feel that bad."

"Nah. I've had three customers since noon. It's not like they're lined up out the door. I'll see you later. Go back to sleep if you want to."

"Okay. See you when you get home." I set the phone down in a daze, still staring at the computer.

I had to try it. I had to. I pulled the chair out and sat down, jiggling the mouse to wake up the screen. Then I pulled up the browser and typed in the same web address I'd used earlier. My blood was pounding in my ears when the home page popped up. My hand shook as I held it over the mouse, going to the *quick search* option. Once again, I clicked the box marked *male* and then went to the drop-down box for *state*. All the way to the very end of the list, the next-to-last option. Wisconsin. In the *missing __ years* space, I put "four." Then I hit the Search button.

Instantly it took me to a page with five pictures on it. Two very familiar faces smiled at me.

Jack and Sam.

Chapter 17

O nly it didn't say Jack and Sam. Jack's picture was the top one, the very first of the five. But beside his picture, the name said Tyler Makovec. Age now: nine. Missing from: Madison, WI. Missing since: January 3 of last year.

Below his picture was Sam's, except the name beside it was Ryan Makovec. Age now: seven. Missing from: Madison, WI. Missing since: January 3. One whole year and nine months.

A real long time.

They looked younger in the pictures, their hair was shorter, and Sam still had his front baby teeth. But it was definitely them. Jack and Sam. Or Tyler and Ryan. No wonder I hadn't found them the first time I looked.

I couldn't believe it. I honestly couldn't believe it. My breath came out in short gasps. I sat there staring at the screen, looking at the pictures that were unmistakably them. My palms felt sweaty. I rubbed them on my cargo shorts to dry them off.

There was a link next to their pictures that said *View Poster*. I clicked on it and a new window opened. Now there were three huge pictures spread across the page in front of me, of both the boys and their father. At the top, in bold letters, it said **Family Abduction**. All the pictures were in color and I could practically count the freckles sprinkled across all three of their faces. Jack was smiling slightly in the shy way he had. Sam had a huge grin on his face. The boys' pictures looked like school photos, but the picture of their father was a candid shot, his head turned a little to the side, his chin tilted and his eyes looking sideways, like he was talking to someone just outside the frame. But he had red hair and freckles and a thick neck. Definitely the guy I'd watched through the binoculars.

Beside each of their pictures was all their information— date of birth, height, weight, race, sex, hair and eye color. Under the pictures was this paragraph: *Tyler and Ryan were abducted by their non-custodial father, Steven Makovec. A felony warrant for Kidnapping has been issued for Steven. Tyler has a small scar below his hairline.*

He did? I looked at Jack's picture, and in it I could see a little white scar at the very top of his forehead. I'd never noticed it before. I studied all the dates and numbers. Jack's—Tyler's— current age was nine, but his date of birth was September 30, just weeks away. He had a September birthday like me. Steven's height was 5 foot 7 —I'd sure pegged that one. His age was twenty-seven, which seemed really young for a dad of two boys. All three of my parents were in their mid-forties.

At the very bottom of the poster, it said *Anyone Having Information Should Contact National Center for Missing & Exploited Children.*

An 800 number was below that.

My eyes darted to the phone on the desk beside me like it was a rattlesnake ready to strike. I'd always thought that if I was ever in a situation where I needed to save someone, I'd act quickly. Jump right in and do what needed to be done. But the phone sat there inches away from my reach and I could not move my hand to pick it up.

I should call Rick. I should tell him this whole crazy, insane story and maybe he'd close up the store right now and come home. This was an emergency, wasn't it?

Now calm down, Chase. Just take it easy, I could hear him saying. Maybe he'd want to wait till Mom got home and then the two of them would talk everything over, look at the website over my shoulder, and ask me fifty million questions.

How long have you known these boys? And you think this was the same guy who stole the lures? Why didn't you tell us about this sooner?

I propped my elbows on the edge of the computer desk and held my head in my hands. I had to tell somebody. I should call, or…do something. I'd just seen them *two* days ago! If I called the 800 number right this second, maybe someone could find them. They were probably still in the state. They might even still be in the county. I could be the hero, the one who found the missing kids and helped them get home again.

I looked at the phone. All I had to do was pick it up and punch in the numbers. *Hello? Yes, I'd like to report a sighting. Tyler and Ryan Makovec from Madison, Wisconsin. I live in Greer, Arizona, and I saw them two days ago. I'm a hundred percent sure it's them.*

But my fingers would not move from the keyboard. I clicked on the Google search window and typed in "Tyler Ryan Makovec." Maybe there were newspaper articles or something that might tell me a little more about them.

133

The very first hit was a website called TylerandRyan.com.

Help Me Find My Children! The headline scrolled continuously across the page. In the center was a picture of the two boys sitting in front of a Christmas tree. They were wearing matching flannel pajamas with bears all over them, and they both held candy canes. A caption underneath said that this was the last picture taken of them before they disappeared with their father in early January of last year.

I spent some time exploring the website. It took me about fifteen seconds to figure out that their mother, Laura Patterson, was not dead. Not only was she alive and well, she'd been desperately looking for them since they were taken by their dad. She had put up this website to try to find them. There were all kinds of pictures of the boys at various ages, lots of them with their mom.

She even had a blog. The entries were all written as if she were writing letters to Tyler and Ryan. The last one was dated just a couple of weeks ago.

Sept. 2

Dear Tyler and Ryan,

I can't believe it—another summer is over and school is starting. Tyler, you're in 4th grade now!! And Ryan, you're already in 2nd. Just think—that's as old as Tyler was the last time I saw you. I bet you guys are so big now!! I hope you like your school and your teachers. I hope you're learning a lot and making new friends. There are so many things I wonder about. Like do you ride a bus to school now or are you close enough to walk? Do you buy your lunches or does Daddy pack a lunch for you? What kind of backpacks did you pick out when you went to buy school stuff this year? And Rye-rye, do you still like Blues Clues or are you too big for that now?

Hide and Seek

I cupped my head in my hands, pressing in with my palms till I thought my skull would explode. I'd told Rick I had a sore throat, and now it really was aching—that pain you get when you're about to cry.

I went back to the home page and read the caption under the Christmas picture again. *Our last Christmas together was such a happy time! My two boys are my most precious treasure. Please help me find my children.*

And then suddenly I grabbed the phone and started punching in the number that was plastered all over the website. It rang four times before a woman's voice answered.

"Hello?"

I hadn't planned what I was going to say. The phone felt slippery in my hot grasp and I pressed it hard against my ear.

"Hello? Who is this?" the voice asked.

In a panic, I hung up and tossed the phone on the futon by the desk. Then I covered it with a pillow. I exited out of the website and raced down the hall to my room. I threw myself onto my bed, my chest heaving.

"Get a grip! What's wrong with you?" I said out loud.

And then the phone rang.

I sat there and listened to the first three rings before I even got off the bed. Finally I jumped up. My shoulder smacked against the door frame as I rushed back to the office to find the buried phone.

When I looked at the handset, I saw that it was the exact same number I'd just dialed. For a half second, I started not to answer it. But then I pushed the talk button.

I paused and cleared my throat. "Hello?"

"Ah, yes, h-hi there," a woman's voice stuttered. "I was... did someone from this number just try to call me?"

"Yeah, that was me. Is this..." My mind blanked and I

couldn't remember the lady's name. Lauren something? "Are you Jack—are you Tyler and Ryan's mom?" I clutched the slippery phone in my fist.

"Yes?" Her voice rose with a hopefulness I could hear right over the phone.

"Um, I'm pretty sure I saw your sons."

Chapter 18

The woman started sobbing. But it was a happy sound too, like she was more relieved than she'd ever been in her life. I paused for a second and waited for her to say something, but when she didn't, I started talking.

I gave her my name and told her I lived in Greer, Arizona. "It's about four hours from Phoenix—up in the mountains. The first time I saw them was...Saturday." Wow—Saturday? Was that the first time I'd seen them? That was just a few days ago. "They're camping out with their father. But they're gone now. I'm not sure where...."

"Gone? Gone where?" she practically screamed.

"I don't know. Yesterday when I went to visit them, they'd packed up their campsite and they were gone."

"Are they okay? Are you sure it's them? Did you see both of them? Did you see their father? Are they healthy and everything?"

"Yeah, I'm sure it's them. I saw their pictures on the missing children website and I have no doubt it's them. Except they told me their names were Jack and Sam."

"Jack and Sam? Oh, how strange! Honey, how old are you?" she asked suddenly, sounding just like a mom.

"Fourteen."

She made that sobbing sound again. "You're so sweet to call," she said, choking on the words. "Do you think I could talk to your parents?"

"Uh, actually, they're not home right now." I paused, trying to think of what to say. "Anyway, my parents don't know anything about this. I just figured it out a few minutes ago myself."

"Where did you say they were now?" she asked, and so I started at the beginning, telling her a shortened version of what had been going on for the past week. I told her I'd been out exploring on my mountain bike and had seen them in the woods. They showed me their campsite and said they were with their dad.

I didn't mention that they were hungry, but I did tell her about bringing them candy. I also left out the part about them thinking she was dead. The poor lady could only deal with five or six shocks at one time, I figured. I tried to assure her that they were healthy. And I didn't go into a lot of details about how it seemed like they didn't really live anywhere and they hadn't been going to school. For now, all she needed to know was that her sons were okay. Then I told her that when I saw them on Monday for the last time, they'd said they were probably leaving soon.

"I'm going to call the detective who's been working with me as soon as we hang up. Hon, can you give me your name again and your parents' names? And can I get your address?"

"Uh, sure," I said, realizing there was no turning back now. I gave her all the information she asked me for and she read it back to me to make sure she had everything right.

"Chase, thank you so, so much for calling! This is the

phone call I've been waiting for. After all these months, I can't believe this is finally happening!"

"Uh, yeah. Me neither," I said.

"I'm sure the detective will want to talk to you. Is this the best number to reach you?"

"Yes," I said, my mind going a hundred miles a minute. Now I'd definitely have to tell Mom and Rick.

She asked me a few more questions and I answered her in a daze. I couldn't believe this was really happening. All along I'd thought something wasn't right with those kids, and now....

We finally hung up. My ear was hurting from the way I'd pressed the phone against it. I slumped into the office chair and stared at the blank computer screen.

Wow. Wow! Kidnapped by their father. Missing for over a year and a half. And he'd been shoplifting stuff they needed and switching out license plates and...who knew what else he'd been up to! He'd even changed their names!

How totally weird was that? What if my dad had one day packed up the three of us and thrown a tent in the trunk of his Lexus? I actually started laughing nervously at the thought of it.

You know what? I've never really thought of you as Chase. From now on, let's call you...Fred. And Kendra, you look more like a... Susan, and Shea, you'll be...Beth. Oh, and by the way, hate to break it to you, but Mom's dead.

Now I'd stopped laughing and I was shaking. A hard shiver, like I was on the verge of freezing to death. It was like my body temperature had suddenly dropped thirty degrees. I couldn't make myself stop. I rubbed my hands up and down my arms and legs, but it didn't help. I leaped out of the chair and started doing jumping jacks. It was insane, but I had to do *something*.

Then all of a sudden I stopped and stood frozen in place. In my mind, I heard sirens blaring, half a dozen police cars surrounding the white pickup. And two little faces staring out from the windshield, their worst nightmare coming true: the bad guys coming to take them away from their dad.

OH MY GOD! I had to find them! I had to! I had to tell them what was going on. Your mother's alive! She's looking for you! The cops aren't bad guys—they're going to take you to your mom!

Yeah, back to your mom but away from your dad. This really was a nightmare.

If only I could find them! I could explain it all to them… or try to, anyway.

Maybe…maybe if I could find them, I could even convince them to come home with me. Maybe I could have Rick and Mom help me look for them in the car, and then they could stay with us until the cops came and we'd call their mom on the phone, and they'd hear her voice and know she was alive, and we'd convince them that everything…everything was going to be okay.

I grabbed the phone again. Should I call Mom and Rick? But it would take too long to tell them everything. Instead I hit redial. This time it didn't even ring before the mom picked up.

"Hello?"

"Hi, this is Chase calling from Arizona again." I still couldn't remember what her name was, but I just kept talking really fast. "I was just thinking…I don't know where they are exactly, but they might have just moved to another campsite near here. And if I could—"

"Oh, Chase. I'm sorry, I'm on the other line with the detective right now. Can I call you back in a few minutes?"

"Uh, sure. It's just…can you tell me something that only Jack, I mean, only Tyler and Ryan would know? Like the name of your dog or something? In case I find them, I want to convince them that I really talked to their mom."

"Oh. Uh…well, Tyler always slept with a teddy bear named Fluppy. Tell him Fluppy's waiting here for him. He's a white bear and he got him for Christmas when he was two. Ryan had a stuffed raccoon that was his favorite. And ask them if they remember the song I used to sing to them—'Beautiful Boy.'" She started singing a few words to it, and humming the tune.

"Okay, thanks! I'll talk to you later. Bye!"

I hung up the phone and raced to my room for my backpack, then barreled down the wooden stairs in three leaps.

"Come on, Dexter! We're on a mission!"

Chapter 19

By the time I got my bike out of the shed and took off down the road, I'd already come up with a plan. I thought about it logically. If they were leaving town, they'd more than likely take the 373 to the 260. That was the main highway that would either take them east to Show Low or west to Springerville. It wasn't the only way out of town, but it was definitely the main road. I figured it was worth a try.

I was desperate to find them and let them know what was about to happen. I couldn't stand the thought of them being scared out of their minds when the cops finally tracked them down. I was pedaling at top speed and in no time at all we were at Sheep's Crossing. Naturally, Dexter veered off to go in that direction. "Not this time, Dext. Keep going. We may have a long ride ahead of us."

We sped along the 373, with me keeping a lookout for the red bandana the whole time. We'd already passed the turnoff for the reservoirs, and I realized once again that the odds were against me finding them. But I had to do something. I couldn't sit at home and wait. I'd be too jumpy. At least this way I was taking some action.

Hide and Seek

It wasn't long until I had to slow down because I was getting tired out, and so was Dexter. How far could I go on my bike? Ten, maybe even twenty miles? But I had to remember that however far I went down the highway, I'd have the whole ride back to make too. And it was already late afternoon, so I only had a couple of hours of daylight. But I did have my flashlight in my backpack, and also my GPS.

"Should we turn back?" I asked Dexter. He trotted along with his mouth open, glad for the fresh air and exercise. The thing was, I figured if I gave up now and went home and told my parents the whole story, they'd tell me it would be ridiculous for us to try to find them.

We have no idea where they're going. Let the police handle this, Chase. It's out of our hands.

They'd think my red bandana idea was stupid, even though they'd never say that out loud.

We slowed to an easy pace, and my eyes scanned the trees. I didn't want to give up. I kept hoping that I'd go just a little farther down the road, and boom, the white pickup would be right in front of me. Or maybe I'd suddenly see Jack and Sam come darting from behind some trees. Maybe, just maybe....

I was really starting to get tired. I had no idea how far we'd gone either. I'd been in such a rush I hadn't bothered to turn on my GPS to track my distance. It felt like miles.

I pedaled and pedaled. Even though it was nice and cool right now, my backpack was making my back sweat, so I wiggled my shoulders to try to shift it around. My lower back was starting to ache, too, from being bent over in one position for so long. I sat up and pumped for a while with my hands on my thighs, carefully balancing my bike. Then I sat forward in the seat and propped my palms on my handlebars.

I almost went right past it. In fact, I did go past it, but something made me stop and do a U-turn.

There, tied to a scraggly branch of a small ponderosa pine, was a red bandana! I braked so hard I left a long skid mark on the pavement behind me.

The red bandana! I wasn't seeing things! There it was, exactly like I'd told him, tied to the branch of a tree. The tree was beside a forest service road—a bare dirt road that would probably lead me to their campsite!

"Jack! Sam!" I yelled at the top of my lungs. I didn't even think about how their dad might be with them now and could hear me too. I was so excited I could hardly contain myself. I got off my bike and pushed it over to the tree to untie the bandana.

Now for the beads. I walked slowly along the dirt road, pushing my bike and scanning the ground. I almost yelled again when I saw a little purple bead in the dirt. They were somewhere close by! My eyes strained as I walked down the road, looking for another bead. Dexter came over and stomped around next to me with his gigantic paws.

"Hey, watch out! You could be stepping all over the beads." It took what seemed like an hour to spot the next bead, about fifteen feet farther down. Only two beads so far. I kept walking and staring at the ground. Finally, I saw a third. More walking, with me pushing my bike along slowly and Dexter sniffing at the trees that lined the road. But after the third, I didn't see any more beads. Birds had probably seen the shiny things in the dirt and taken them away, because I sure wasn't finding any more. Okay, maybe leaving a trail of beads hadn't been such a bright idea after all.

But I knew they were close by. Or at least they had been within the past two days. I cupped my hands over my mouth and yelled. "Jack! Sam!" Their dad might hear me too, but it was a chance I had to take. I walked a little farther down the road, hoping to catch a glimpse of a tent. "Jack! Sam!"

Dexter gazed at me with his head slightly tilted. "Don't just look at me; help me out here." I slapped my thighs to try to get him excited so he'd start barking. It worked, and while I yelled for Jack and Sam, Dexter barked.

I paused to listen.

"Jack! Sam!"

And then I heard it—*the duck call!* Dexter heard it too, turning his head in the direction it'd come from, through the trees on the right side of the dirt road. "Jack! Sam!" I yelled, dropping my bike by the side of the road and running in that direction. Again came the call, louder this time. We were getting closer!

"Jack! Sam!" I yelled, and Dexter ran ahead of me. I hoped he'd take me right to them. Ahead of us in the trees I heard the crashing sound of someone running through the underbrush and then a short toot on the duck call.

"Keep blowing! I can hear you!" I yelled. And then there was movement, and the next minute, Jack was racing up to me and grabbing me around the waist so hard we both almost fell over.

"Hey, buddy!" I shouted. He still had me around the waist in a death grip. "I can't believe it! I found you! The red bandana worked!" I was so excited, and I had a million things to tell him—how I'd seen the bandana, and how the beads didn't end up helping much, and about his mom. And his teddy bear and the song.

Jack looked up at me with his eyes wide. He hadn't said a word or even made a sound. "Where's Sam?" I asked him. Something in his expression made all the blood in my body drain down to my toes. "What's up? Everything okay?"

Jack shook his head quickly. His face was tense and his eyes were the size of two car headlights.

"Where's your brother?" I asked again. I tried to sound calm, but the look on his face was scaring me to death.

"Sick," Jack said finally, his voice hoarse. "You got to help him."

Chapter 20

Where is he?" I asked.

Jack pointed down the road. "In the tent. Will you help us?"

"Of course. Let's go see him." Jack grabbed me by the hand and pulled me along. He was squeezing my hand so tight it actually hurt a little, but I kept quiet. A second ago he'd come crashing through the trees, but now he led me farther down the dirt road. In his other hand he was still gripping the duck call.

Then we came to a spot by the side of the road where the tent was set up, but none of the other camping gear was around and the truck wasn't there either. "Where's your dad?" I asked.

"Gone to get medicine. Sam's in here." Jack bent down and ducked under the tent flaps, so I followed him.

Instantly, the stench hit me—the strong smell of vomit. I tried to hold my breath and act like it didn't bother me. It was dark inside the tent. Warm, stuffy air hung over everything. Sam was lying curled up on a bare air-mattress with his eyes closed and a bunch of blankets piled down around his feet.

He had no shirt on, just a pair of jeans. His hair was all damp and sweaty, and I could hear his breath coming heavily out of his open mouth.

Dexter had followed us in, and he circled anxiously a few times and went right back out again. I wished I could follow him. Here I was, with a real chance to be a hero, and all I could think about was getting out of here.

Jack knelt on the edge of the air mattress. "Sam? Chase is here. He found us. He's going to help us."

I swallowed, feeling like there was absolutely nothing I could do at that moment that might be helpful. Sam's eyelids fluttered a little and he opened his eyes.

"Hey, buddy," I said softly to him. "What's up? You sick?"

"Um," Sam grunted a little. I noticed a cooking pot next to the air mattress, and the smell of vomit grew even stronger. I quickly looked away from it.

"Been throwing up, huh?" I asked, bending down beside him. Sam made the grunting sound again. Except for opening his eyes and turning his head a little, he hadn't moved. He stayed curled up in a ball, his knees almost to his chest.

Jack looked at me with terror in his eyes. "You got to help him."

"How long has he been like this?" I put my hand on his bare arm, and I could feel how hot his skin was.

"Uh, since yesterday…I think. When we were packing up to leave, he said he had a stomachache. Dad said he was just faking it so he wouldn't have to help. Then Sam started throwing up when we were in the truck. Dad said he was car sick, but he kept throwing up and he wouldn't eat anything. We were on our way to someplace warm. With an ocean. But we had to stop because Sam got sick. Dad's in a bad mood now."

I let out a slow breath. "Sam, do you hurt anywhere?"

Sam looked at me and nodded. "My stomach. Really bad."

Jack squeezed my arm. "Can you do something for him?"

I looked at Sam and then at Jack. I'd never seen such a sick kid before. He was barely moving. What could I possibly do to help him? I wished I could pull some magic vial out of my pocket and give it to him, and he'd sit up and grin at me and ask for candy.

I couldn't even tell what was wrong with him, except that he was in really bad shape. What would my parents do for me if I was like this?

"He needs a doctor," I said finally.

Jack shook his head quickly. "No. Dad's getting him some medicine."

I looked back at Sam's pinched little face. "But he's really, really sick, Jack. It could be serious." I sat there, thinking. "Hold on a second." I crawled out of the tent and grabbed my backpack where I'd left it just outside, relieved to breathe in cool, fresh air around me. I took out my GPS and turned it on, waiting for it to pick up the satellites. Then I marked this spot as a waypoint.

I'd go home and get Mom and Rick to come back here with the car. We could drive the boys into Springerville to the emergency room. I glanced at Dexter lying under the trees nearby. If only I could just send him back alone with a note attached to his collar.

I heard a retching sound and Jack's face appeared between the tent flaps. "He's throwing up again!"

"Okay, I'm coming." I slipped the GPS into my pocket and ducked back inside the dark tent. Sam was leaning over the pot.

"It hurts!" he moaned, clutching his stomach. I wondered

if he had food poisoning or something. But did people run fevers with that? All I knew was that he was really sick and needed more help than I could give him.

"Can you get him some water?" I asked Jack, looking around the shadowy tent. Jack scooted over to the corner and used a plastic gallon jug of water to fill up a blue tin cup.

He gave it to me and I held it up to Sam's mouth. He shook his head and collapsed back on the air mattress. "Just a few sips," I told him. He turned his head and I held the cup for him and let him drink a little.

"Listen, Jack. I'm going to go get help. I'll bring my mom and stepfather back here, and they'll be able to help Sam. But it'll take me a little while to—"

"No! Don't leave! You've got to help us!" Jack grabbed my arm with both hands, his fingernails digging into my skin.

"I am going to help you. I promise I'll come right back, but I'll have to leave to go get—"

Suddenly Dexter's bark went off like an alarm, making both of us jump. It was deafening and he wouldn't stop.

Jack peeked through the flaps of the tent. "My dad's here! He's back!" He looked over his shoulder at me and all the blood seemed to drain out of his face.

I felt trapped, crouching inside the tent. An outsider, a snoop. What would he do when he found me? I thought about ducking under the back of the tent and trying to escape that way.

But I sat there frozen. Dexter kept barking his head off.

"Jack!" I heard a man's voice yell. He sounded really mad. Or at least surprised.

Jack disappeared through the tent flaps and I decided to follow him. At the very least I had to make Dexter shut up.

Hide and Seek

His constant barking ricocheted around the trees and bounced back to my eardrums.

As soon as I popped out of the hot tent, I was practically face to face with the dad. His face was flaming red and, up close, his muscular arms and broad chest made him look massive. He had a rifle in one hand. The driver's door of the truck was still open.

"Who's this guy?" the dad bellowed at me while Dexter barked like a mad dog.

"Dexter, quiet!"

"What's going on here?" He took a step in my direction. Dexter bared his teeth and snarled ferociously.

"Dexter, cut it out!" I shouted. Jack was trying to tell his dad something, but who could hear over all the noise?

"I'll shut him up!" the man yelled, raising the rifle and pointing it right at my dog.

"No! Don't!"

I raced forward, trying to grab the gun—

The world went dark.

Chapter 21

Bounce, bounce, bounce. Shea was sitting on my bed, bouncing. Trying to wake me up. *Leave me alone, Shea.* Bounce, bounce, bounce. *Leave me alone.* Bounce, bounce. I wanted to sleep. A deep, deep sleep like being underwater. But she wouldn't stop bouncing. *Can't you just let me sleep?* The bed shook and shook.

In my head I was telling Shea to leave me alone. *Stop it, Shea.* But she couldn't hear me. I couldn't make my voice work. Why wouldn't she stop bouncing!

"Stop it." There. I'd said that out loud. But it sounded like *sssss.* Air coming out of a balloon. *Sssssss.* "Stop," I tried again, louder. It came out, "Ah." Man, was I tired.

"Shea." I heard a voice say her name out loud. Was that my voice? My leg reached out. I'd kick her off the bed. That would make her stop. My foot hit something hard. "Let me sleep!" I moaned. My face was smushed against the bed, which was so hard. And cold.

My head rolled around on the pillow. It was hard too. God, this bed was uncomfortable.

My head hurt.

And the bed was still shaking.

I forced my eyelids open. Everything was dark. Where was Shea? I could still feel the bouncing. I strained my eyes to look for my alarm clock. Why was my bed moving? "Mom?" There was stuff piled all around me. Who put this stuff on my bed? I rubbed my eyes.

Everything was spinning. The room was moving.

No, wait. The *truck* was moving.

I twisted my head around, but the second I moved, my skull felt like it was splitting open. I was in the back of the pickup, in the camper part. Behind me was the cab, and I could see two dark outlines—one big and one little. A glass window separated me from them. The dashboard glowed a soft green.

A rifle was hanging from a gun rack on the other side of the glass.

A rifle.

I lay back down on the hard metal of the truck bed. It was starting to come back to me. Jack and me inside the tent. Sam sick. The dad. A rifle. Dexter wouldn't stop barking.

Dexter! Where was Dexter? I sat up a little and looked around me, half expecting to see his dark form panting in the corner of the truck. He'd come over and bump against me and breathe his warm dog breath on me and let me know everything was fine.

But Dexter wasn't there.

I strained to remember. Had I heard a rifle go off? Had there been a shot?

What had happened? I rubbed my forehead and instantly felt a throbbing pain. Tenderly, my fingers touched a lump the size of a golf ball. Ouch, that hurt! Could that really be on my head? It was huge! And so, so sore. Cautiously, I traced around the lump with one finger. I couldn't feel a cut or anything, just an egg-sized knot.

Did I fall down? Did I get hit in the head? Did the rifle go off? *What was I doing here?* Did I get in this truck by myself or did...someone throw me in here? I couldn't remember anything.

The truck was driving over rough ground. Wherever we were, we weren't on a paved road. I could tell that much by the way the truck bounced up and down on its shocks. The throbbing in my head seemed to be in rhythm with the bouncing of the truck. All around me were dark shapes, and I carefully—quietly—reached out to explore my surroundings. I didn't want to make too much noise and draw attention to myself.

The stuff around me felt like piles of camping gear. Something folded up and slick was under my foot—a tarp or something. A couple of boxes and plastic containers full of stuff. Was my backpack in here? I couldn't see anything. I felt around for about ten minutes and never came across anything that felt like my backpack.

I looked out the camper windows. It was starting to get dark outside. What time was it? Had I only been out for a few minutes? Or more like an hour?

I lay flat in the bed of the pickup with my arm under my head to cushion it from the bouncing. Where were they going? *And why were they taking me with them?* What was this man going to do to me?

Wait. Jack had told me something about where they were going. I tried to remember what he said, but it was like walking through fog. Water. Warm. They were on their way to a warm place. Ocean. Did he say they were going to the ocean, or did I just imagine that part? I was pretty sure he'd said they were going someplace with an ocean.

California. Or Mexico. Which direction were we going? If it was light outside, I could figure that out. If we were heading to California, we'd be going west. Mexico was south. Once the sun came up, I could tell which way we were going.

But I couldn't wait that long! I had to get out of this truck somehow. How fast were we going? Not too fast because we were bouncing along this unpaved road. We probably weren't going more than fifteen miles an hour.

Could I crawl to the rear of the truck and climb out over the tailgate? Jump out and then take off running? Would I break my leg? What if they heard me escaping?

I craned my neck around to get a look inside the cab again. All I could see were the two outlines I'd seen before. There was a dark form against the passenger door. Maybe that was Sam. The small outline had to be Jack. The big outline of their dad was staring straight ahead.

I could try it now. Creep to the back of the truck, open the camper door and crawl out, and then jump, like doing a cannonball into a pool, with my legs balled up underneath me, and I'd land hard but hopefully I wouldn't break anything, then I'd run as fast as I could, away from the maniac with the rifle.

I was going to have to crawl over some of this camping gear and I had to be quiet, or he'd hear me and stop the truck, and then what? I sat up slowly and glanced over my shoulder one more time. The big outline hadn't moved; it still stared straight ahead.

I began to scoot forward until I felt something in front of my hands. It felt like a box, and I was about to slide it out of my way when I felt the truck speeding up. The bumping stopped, and we started moving faster, traveling down a paved road. I could feel it.

I tried looking out the windows of the camper, but in the fading light I could only see outlines of things as we sped past them. I must've been knocked out for a while, because it had been just before sunset when Jack and I were in the tent with Sam, and now the light was fading fast.

I had to get out of here! But I couldn't jump out now; we were going too fast. How was I going to get away? I'd have to wait till the truck stopped, or at least slowed down. How long would that be?

I lay down, feeling the rhythm of the wheels against the highway. My head hurt, and I couldn't think straight. My eyelids grew heavy from the gentle movement of the truck as it sped along the road, taking us…somewhere. I tried to keep them open, but I just felt so tired.

I should stay awake. Pay attention to my surroundings. Stay…alert.

* * *

I wasn't sure how much later it was when I felt the truck make a turn. I opened my eyes but the camper was completely dark. We were bouncing along an unpaved road again. How long had I been asleep? I sat up and looked at the outlines on the other side of the glass. Jack's head lay back on the seat like he was sleeping. I could just see the top of Sam's head, too, leaning against the passenger door.

If we were back on an unpaved road, did that mean we'd be stopping soon? Maybe I should try to make a break for it—crawl to the back of the truck and force the camper door open.

But I lay unmoving, feeling the truck bounce along. Where were we? How far from home was I now?

Ten minutes passed, maybe more. The truck lurched a little and I braced myself to keep from sliding across the truck bed.

Then we came to a stop. I heard the sound of the emergency brake being applied. The engine was turned off and, almost like it was in my ear, a man's voice said, "Wake up. We're stopping for a while."

Chapter 22

I flattened myself against the truck bed. What should I do? Make a run for it? Play dead? Hit him with something heavy when he opened up the back?

I lay still, waiting to see what would happen. I heard the cab door open and close. Felt the truck rock slightly with the slamming of the door. I should run now! No, it was too late. He'd catch me. Maybe even shoot at me.

I heard the back of the camper open, and a beam of light bounced across the contents of the camper bed. I blinked and covered my eyes with my arm. The light moved down so it wasn't blinding me, and I lowered my arm to look up. All I could see was the dark outline of a man holding a flashlight.

"You awake?" a gruff voice said. I wasn't sure if he was talking to me so I kept quiet and didn't move.

"Hey! You hear me back there?" the voice asked, louder this time. The beam of the flashlight danced across my face and chest.

"I hear you," I said finally, blinking from the light. I tried to make my voice sound strong so he wouldn't hear how scared I was.

"Come on out," he ordered, shining the light on the cargo in front of me so I could see to climb over it.

Slowly I moved around all the gear till I was at the back of the truck. I saw a little shadow by his side. Jack. I wondered where Sam was.

As I swung one leg over the tailgate, I hesitated for a second. I could feel something heavy shift inside the pocket of my cargo shorts, like a weight.

My GPS! My GPS was in my pocket! I could find my way out of here! Just as soon as I could get away.

I climbed out of the truck and stood in front of the dad. He shone the flashlight in my face and I squinted until he finally lowered it, pointing the beam at the ground.

"You—you okay?" he asked. His voice sounded scared. Was he scared of me?

"I guess."

There was a long pause. "I thought maybe…I wasn't sure if I'd killed you back there," he said softly. I looked up at him, but in the dark I couldn't really read his expression. Was he relieved he hadn't killed me? Or disappointed? Jack stood at his elbow, but I couldn't see his face very well either.

"What are we doing here?" I asked finally.

His hand went up and rubbed his face. "I got to figure this out. We need to—I got to sleep first." He stood there in the darkness, not moving.

As soon as I'd stepped out into the night air, I'd expected it to be chilly, but it wasn't at all. It was actually really warm, and I felt comfortable in just my T-shirt and cargo shorts.

My head was throbbing from the pain, but I couldn't do anything about that now. I looked around, trying to figure out where we were. It was pitch-black out here; the only light to see by was the beam of the flashlight. Wherever we were, there weren't any streetlights nearby. And I had a feeling we hadn't been driving on a paved road for a while.

"Give me a hand," the dad said. I wasn't sure if he was talking to me or not. He and Jack lowered the tailgate and started pulling things out. I stayed put, not sure what was expected of me.

What was he going to do? Take me with them to California? Or Mexico? I had to get out of here, find some way to get to a phone, or flag down a passing car so I could call my parents. They must be out of their minds with worry right now.

The guy had turned on a camping lantern and set it on the opened tailgate, so now a little pool of light lit up the back of the truck. He turned off the flashlight and laid it next to the lantern. "Just the sleeping bags," he told Jack. "We're not gonna be here long enough to mess with the tent."

"What about the air mattresses?" Jack asked.

"No. Don't bother with them either."

They pulled out three rolled-up sleeping bags and tossed them on the ground. I stood still, my arms crossed, but the whole time I kept my eye out for my backpack while they rummaged through the stuff in the truck bed. I didn't see it, though, and while Jack unrolled the sleeping bags, his dad went to the passenger side of the cab and came back carrying Sam in his arms. He laid Sam on a sleeping bag spread out on the ground. For a second I thought he was dead, until he moaned a little and rolled over. He looked so pale, but he was sleeping soundly now.

"He needs a doctor," I said, but my voice came out raspy and I didn't sound very brave. I sounded young, like a scared little boy.

I hated sounding like that. I wished this guy would take me seriously. Maybe even be afraid of me. Or at least respect me. But I was just a kid to him. And my head hurt, and part of me really wished I had my mom right now.

"Just keep quiet," he told me over his shoulder. "He's alright. He's sleeping. That's what I need. We all just need some sleep. And then I can figure this thing out." After he put Sam down, he headed back toward the cab of the truck.

"No, he's sick! He needs a doctor!" I said, louder this time. It scared me to speak up like that, but I hated that he thought I was just some wimp kid.

Suddenly the guy turned and got right in my face. "Shut up! You've caused enough trouble already!" I could smell the stink of stale cigarettes on his breath. Jack stood silent and unmoving in the shadows next to Sam. He hadn't said a word to me since the truck had stopped.

"What are you going to do to me? You have to let me go!" I yelled.

He raised his fist like he was going to hit me, but then he grabbed his head with his hands. "Watch it, kid!" he bellowed at me in a rage. "I haven't slept in two days, I got a sick boy to deal with, and then you show up and get in the way! I thought I'd killed you back there! I can't think straight! I CAN'T THINK!"

I stood frozen in place. This crazy man literally looked like he was about to pull his hair out, the way he clutched his head in his hands like that. He was breathing hard and rocking back and forth a little. I didn't dare make a move. At first he sounded scared, or at least sorry that he'd hurt me. Now he was losing it right in front of me. Was the guy really unstable? Or just exhausted out of his mind?

After a minute or so he seemed to calm down. He took a deep breath and stepped past me. He went to the cab of the truck, coming back with the rifle.

I dropped my hands to my sides and felt my knees go weak. For a second I thought I might actually faint. Was he going to shoot me right here? Should I start begging for my life? He'd tried to shoot my dog. For all I knew, Dexter might be—

I wouldn't let my mind go there.

"I don't want any trouble from you. Got that?" he said. He held the gun at his side with the barrel pointing toward the ground, but the message was clear.

I nodded but I couldn't make my voice work. To think I'd once felt sorry for this guy. Thought he was homeless, thought he might need *my* help. What an idiot I'd been.

He walked over to Jack and handed him the rifle. "You're on guard duty. I gotta sleep. You hear me? I have to sleep!" His voice rose with emotion. "You better keep quiet and let me get some rest or there'll be big trouble! You only wake me up if there's an emergency. Got that?"

"Yes, sir!" said Jack, sounding like a soldier who'd just gotten his orders. I'd never heard him sound so tough before. His dad grabbed him by both shoulders. "I'm counting on you. Don't let me down."

"I won't."

My heart thumped with a sudden rush of blood. I couldn't believe my luck! He was putting Jack in charge! As soon as his father fell asleep, I could knock him in the head, steal the keys to the truck, and get all three of us out of here!

Or maybe not. But at least I could get away. Jack would help me sneak away, maybe even give me some water if he knew where some was, and with my GPS I could find my way out of here.

"You—come here," he said to me. Trying to be brave, I walked slowly and determinedly over to where he and Jack were standing. He kicked at one of the sleeping bags with his foot. "Sit down."

I sat down cross-legged on the sleeping bag. I was relieved to be sitting, because my headache was making me kind of dizzy, and what I really wanted to do was stretch out on this sleeping bag and fall asleep next to Sam.

"Just don't cause any trouble," he warned me. "Any more than you've already caused."

Then he grabbed one of the sleeping bags and went to the back of the truck. He clicked the flashlight on and turned off the camping lantern sitting on the tailgate. "Don't want to waste these batteries. The flashlight will give you enough light."

He handed the flashlight to Jack and then took the sleeping bag to the cab of the truck. The door opened and closed, and I could hear him moving around in the cab, spreading out the sleeping bag. After a few minutes, everything got quiet.

Okay. So much for my plan to steal the truck and drive away in the night. I let out a long sigh and looked up at Jack, who was still standing in front of me, holding the flashlight in one hand and the rifle in the other. Finally, we were alone. I'd wait until I was sure his father was asleep, and then…freedom!

I patted the sleeping bag next to me, signaling Jack to sit down beside me. He glanced over his shoulder toward the truck and then looked back at me. His face was all shadowy from the soft glow of the flashlight. He shook his head no.

"It's okay," I whispered softly. "Have a seat."

"I'm keeping watch," he whispered back.

"I know. But you don't want to stand up all night do you?"

Jack glanced at Sam curled up asleep near me, and then took a seat on the edge of Sam's sleeping bag, laying the flashlight at his feet so the beam gave off a little glow. At last it was just the three of us again, like usual, even if Sam was totally passed out.

My head felt heavy on my neck, and I wondered if I'd be

able to stay awake for very long. How long should I wait?

From the dim light that the flashlight gave off, I tried to look around and get some idea of our surroundings, but I couldn't really see anything. The sleeping bags were lying on bare ground. I could see a shadowy outline of a rock formation a few feet away from us, but that was all. No trees, no road signs—nothing. Overhead, a zillion stars were in the sky.

The pain in my head seemed to be worse now, like I could feel the blood pulsing through my veins with every beat of my heart. I reached up and touched the knot on my forehead again. "Jack, what happened back there?" I whispered. Then I asked the question I couldn't get out of my mind. "Did your dad...shoot Dexter?"

Jack did his little half-shrug and didn't say anything.

"You have to tell me. Is my dog—is he dead?"

Jack shook his head a little. "He ran off. I didn't see him," he whispered.

I felt relieved to hear that he'd gotten away, but what if he'd been wounded? And he was out in the woods all alone. I tried to convince myself that he'd be able to find his way home.

"What's going to happen to me? Why did he bring me along?" I asked him.

"You didn't move or anything after he hit you."

"Your dad hit me?"

Jack nodded. "Yeah. Like this." He grasped the rifle in both hands and jabbed it in the air. His dad must've hit me with the butt of it.

"What happened after he hit me?"

In the shadowy light, Jack's face tensed. "He kept yelling, 'I think I killed this kid! I think I killed this kid!' Really loud. Sam started crying. Dad freaked out a little bit. He yelled at me to throw everything in the truck so we could get away."

Great—was he planning on dumping my body along the road or something? Good thing I came to before he tried to shovel dirt over me.

"You can live with us now," said Jack. "And we can catch fish and cook them on the little stove. My dad will show you how. He only yells some of the time."

I already have a dad. Two dads. Did I say that out loud? The light was swaying a little.

"Ummm." Sam moaned and then got quiet again. We both glanced at him to see if he was going to wake up, but he let out a long sigh and then his breathing was steady again.

"Is Sam okay?" I whispered.

Jack nodded. "Dad gave him some Tylenol and he fell asleep."

Tylenol might help for a little while, but I doubted it would fix whatever the real problem was. I had to get away, get to a phone to call my parents. And get help for these guys too.

Suddenly everything came rushing back to me—their mom, the website, all the stuff I'd been planning to tell them about till things took such a wrong turn.

"Jack, I have to tell you something," I whispered, but then I couldn't think of how to begin. How should I tell him that his mom was alive, that his dad had stolen him and Sam away from her and had been hiding out with them all this time?

Jack glanced at me. He was holding the rifle across his knees, and I was so relieved that his dad had actually trusted him to be in charge. So relieved that we were alone, and that in just a few minutes I could get out of here and get us help.

"Jack, I have some really good news for you. You're not going to believe it," I whispered to him.

In the dim light of the flashlight, I could see him perking up a little.

As much as I wanted to blurt it right out about his mom, I felt like I should lead up to it so it wouldn't be such a shock.

"You know how you guys told me your names were Jack and Sam? Well, guess what? I found out that your name's really Tyler, isn't it? And Sam's name is Ryan. Tyler and Ryan Makovec. And your dad's name is Steven. Isn't that right?"

Jack sat perfectly still. I could feel his eyes on me, but he didn't make a sound.

"And you used to live in Madison, Wisconsin. That's why Sam—Ryan—said he liked the Packers. Right?" Jack didn't move. The light from the flashlight made him look ghostly white.

"And you have a teddy bear named…" Oh no, I couldn't remember what she'd said. It started with an F, I thought. My brain still felt foggy. "A white teddy bear that you got for Christmas when you were two, and you always slept with it. Well, guess what? It's back at your house in Wisconsin, waiting for you. And Sam—I mean Ryan—slept with a raccoon. And the last time you saw your mom, it was at Christmastime, wasn't it?"

Jack didn't say anything, just stared at me unblinking. It was like he'd turned to stone—a pale little boy statue, frozen there with a rifle across his legs.

I watched for some sign that he was taking all this in, that he was remembering some of this, but there was nothing. I had to keep talking. As soon as I told him about his mother being alive, he'd be so happy he'd let me take off. I'd go running into the night, getting away from here as fast as I could till I could get help. For all of us.

My hand rested gently on the GPS, which I could feel through the cloth of my cargo shorts.

"And your mom used to sing a song to you and Ryan. 'Beautiful Boy.' It went like this." I sang a few of the words, remembering the tune his mother had sung to me over the phone. Jack's face was absolutely blank, his eyes staring not at me but through me, like he couldn't see me anymore. Like he couldn't see anything.

"And you know what else?" I whispered to him, leaning forward a little. I reached out and gently laid my hand on his shoulder. "Your mom is alive, Tyler. I know she is because I talked to her on the phone. She's looking for you and Ryan." It seemed like it was time for me to start using their real names now.

His eyes flickered from side to side like he was reading something. He shot a quick look at Sam curled up on the sleeping bag and then looked back at me.

"I know you thought she was dead. Maybe your dad told you that, but he was...he was wrong. She's alive, and she wants you to come home. She misses you and Ryan so much, Tyler." I let out a slow breath, so relieved to have finally told him what he needed to hear.

He stared at me, unmoving. Any minute now he might start to cry, and I'd tell him everything was going to be okay, and then I could leave.

"You okay? I know it's a big surprise. It's great news, though! Your mom's alive!" I put one hand on his shoulder, and his whole body tensed.

In one sudden movement, he clenched the rifle in both hands and pointed the barrel right at my head. "Shut up! I'll blow your brains out!"

Chapter 23

Now I was the one who'd turned to stone. I didn't move a fraction of a millimeter. I didn't breathe. The barrel of the rifle was six inches from my nose. It swayed ever so slightly in Jack's grip. One flinch, one spasm of his finger... He might not even mean for it to happen.

For eons we were frozen in that spot. Jack's sudden movement had sent the flashlight spinning, and now it lay behind us, the beam of light pointing off into the dark night, leaving us in eerie shadows. But I could see the barrel of the gun. I could feel it hovering in front of my face.

My head throbbed in agony, and now my chest hurt from holding my breath. I opened my mouth and gradually let the trapped air in my lungs out, terrified that this slight movement might set him off. The barrel stared at me with its one black eye. I was barely even aware of Jack on the other end of it, in the shadows.

I took in a shallow breath and I could smell the oily scent of the metal.

I'm going to die. He's going to kill me, and they'll dump my body out here in the middle of nowhere. My parents will never know what happened...

Hide and Seek

I could grab the barrel and point it away, wrench the rifle from his small hands, but could I be fast enough? What if it went off and hit Sam? Or else Steven might wake up and then he'd finish me off for good.

"Jack, put the gun down." How could this be happening? I didn't know this kid Tyler who had suddenly turned on me. But I did know Jack.

The barrel thrust menacingly closer to my face. I leaned back cautiously. I had my hands behind me, propping myself up. I felt the sting of gravel digging into my palms.

"Come on, buddy. Don't hurt me," I begged.

"Liar." Now the barrel was three inches away from me, maybe less.

"Jack, I'm your friend. Don't you know that by now? Remember the food I brought you? And the toys?"

No answer. Sam stirred a little on the sleeping bag beside him.

"I've always helped you. Please, please put the gun down."

The barrel lowered a bit so it wasn't pointing at my face. Now it was aimed at my chest. Not a major improvement.

"All the way down, okay? I know you don't really want to hurt me."

The barrel didn't move.

If only it was light out. If Jack could see me, if I could look into his eyes and talk to him, I didn't think he'd be able to hold me hostage like this.

But it was dark, and he was scared.

He wasn't the only one.

"Uh," groaned Sam. He thrashed suddenly on the sleeping bag, and a high-pitched cry came out of him, like someone stepping on a squeaky toy. The barrel of the rifle dropped a few inches and Jack moved forward, hovering over Sam.

For a split second, I thought about snatching the rifle out of his hands now, while his guard was down. But I didn't. I couldn't do that to him.

My mind was racing. I had to do something to convince him he could trust me.

"He's still really sick," I whispered. "He's been sleeping all this time, but when he wakes up, he'll probably start throwing up again."

Jack didn't move. The rifle wasn't pointed at me now, but I was terrified that one wrong move, one wrong word, could set him off.

Slowly, carefully, I edged over to where the beam of light was coming from. With one hand, I felt around behind me, trying to find the flashlight. I wrapped my fingers around the cool plastic and pulled it toward me so the light was shining on my face.

"Jack, listen. Please let me go and get help. Sam is so sick. He needs more medicine, something to make him stop throwing up. And to get his fever to go down." I was saying all kinds of random things, anything I could think of that might convince him to let me go. "I promise I'll come back with medicine. Don't I keep my promises? The candy, the food—remember? I always bring you what I say I will, don't I?"

Jack now had the rifle lying across his knees again. He'd relaxed a little, but I couldn't take any chances.

"I'll go get some medicine for his stomach and his fever, and I'll come back. If I don't, you can wake up your dad."

Jack's eyes were wide in the glow of the flashlight. It helped that we could see each other now. I kept my eyes on his, talking to him, begging him. "I swear I'll come back. I told you I'd look for you if you tied the bandana to a tree, and it worked, didn't it? I found you, and now I want to help you. I'm your friend."

Jack's eyes darted to Sam and then to the pickup where his father was sleeping. He seemed to have forgotten he even had the rifle in his lap, and I wasn't about to remind him of it.

"I'll only be gone a few minutes. I'll be right back, and then I'll have some medicine for Sam. You can give it to him, and he'll be better." I gently set the flashlight down in front of me. Slowly I started rising to my feet, talking the whole time. "Your dad won't even wake up. You won't even have to tell him I was gone for a little while. That's how fast I'll come back."

Every muscle in my body felt like a tightly wound spring, but I kept my voice calm. "Everything's going to be okay, Jack. You have to believe me." Now I was standing up. I felt the GPS shift slightly in my pocket. I put one foot behind me and took a step backwards.

Jack looked at me. The glow of the flashlight lit up his scared little face. "You'll be right back?"

"Of course I will. I'll be right back. I'm going to help you and Sam." I inched my way out of the circle of light. If I could just get out of the light...

"You stay here and take care of Sam, okay?" Now I'd moved three or four feet away from him, stepping carefully backwards the whole time. "Promise me you'll take care of him?" One step...two...three.

"I promise."

"Okay, I'll be right back."

Every muscle in my body was tensed. I did a slow 180-degree turn, terrified to be turning my back on him. A spot between my shoulder blades prickled; what if he shot me now, in the back? I wanted to run, take off in a lightning sprint until I was out of rifle range. But I forced myself to walk slowly, calmly, quietly.

Rocks and hard-packed dirt crunched under my feet, but I crept along softly, trying not to make much noise. Just get far enough away. Ten feet. Twenty.

I wanted desperately to look over my shoulder, to see if Jack was sitting there in the glow of the flashlight with the rifle pointed at my back. But I didn't dare.

Keep moving. Slow. Careful.

And then I was off. Racing through total blackness, feet pounding against dirt, arms pumping, heart pounding, head throbbing. I ran as fast as I possibly could, gasping to draw in breath, forcing myself to keep moving. I ran till my side was screaming in pain from lack of oxygen. I stumbled over a rock and my ankle buckled. I came so close to losing my balance. My arms flailed out in empty space to brace against the fall.

But I didn't fall. I found my footing again and kept running. My hand reached down and felt the wonderful, heavy weight of the GPS bouncing around in my pocket. The thump of my feet against the ground was the sweetest sound I'd ever heard.

I got away! I got away!

Chapter 24

I ran in a straight line, in almost total darkness. I ran blindly, desperately. I ran till I thought my lungs would explode. I ran till I finally couldn't run anymore. I sank to my knees, feeling gravel scrape against bare skin. I gasped and panted for breath, trying to fill up my aching lungs. My head pounded like a jackhammer.

Only then did I look behind me. Off in the black of the night, I could see a faint little glow. I couldn't tell how far away it was. It was so hard to judge distance in the darkness. I still sat there on my knees, huffing like a racehorse. I knew I should get up and start running again as fast as I could. It was only a matter of time till Jack figured it out. Till he woke up his father. Till they came after me again.

And they'd be in the truck with the headlights shining on me. No matter how much I darted and ducked around trying to escape the headlights, they'd be faster, mowing me down, shooting at me with the rifle.

I rose to my feet and started running again, but this time I didn't go far. I couldn't let myself panic. Stay calm! Make a plan!

I stopped running and dug inside my pocket for my GPS. Thank God! My hands shook as I turned it on. But it didn't go on. I pushed and pushed at the button, but nothing was happening! I realized I was pushing the wrong button.

"Stop it! You can't panic!" I said out loud through gritted teeth.

I pushed the power button and the screen lit up, and as I waited for it to pick up the satellite signals, I caught my breath, glad for this dim little light in the surrounding darkness. Once the GPS was ready to navigate, the first thing I checked was the time. I couldn't believe it; it was only 10:36 p.m.! I'd thought it was the middle of the night.

So I'd been missing for only a few hours. Enough to make Mom and Rick worry, though. Had they called the cops? I was sure they were totally frantic right now. The sooner I got to a phone and called them, the better.

I opened the map page to try to figure out where in the world I was. The icon pointed to a spot in the middle of a totally blank screen. No other landmarks were visible.

"Okay, great. I'm in the middle of nowhere," I muttered out loud. "I already knew that much." I zoomed out five hundred feet, .2 miles, .3 miles, .5 miles—and still nothing. Then when I'd zoomed out to a radius of two miles surrounding my location, a line appeared in the lower right corner of the screen. Finally! A road.

The backlight went off and I turned it on again so I could see. This was the only light I had now. If only I'd grabbed that camping lantern that was sitting on the tailgate. If only I had my backpack with the flashlight inside. If only...a lot of things.

I panned the arrow down to the line at the bottom of the screen and "US 60" popped up. *That's where we were?* US 60?

I knew that highway. It was close to Phoenix! We'd driven all the way to Phoenix?

I pushed the *find* button and chose the *cities* option. Globe, Miami, and Claypool came up. Globe—that was a mining town halfway between Show Low and the eastern edge of the Phoenix Valley. The 60 ran right through it. There were two ways we'd go to visit my dad—most of the time we'd take the 260 all the way to Payson and then take the Beeline Highway into Phoenix. But another route was to take the 60 from Show Low down through all these little old mining towns. And that's the way we'd come. Okay! I knew where I was!

I checked the distance from my current location to the 60, and it was 2.3 miles. I let out a long sigh of relief. I wasn't right by a major highway, but at least it was a manageable walking distance. How far from here to Globe? That was only 4.2 miles! We were practically on the edge of town! That meant people, telephones, rescue!

The backlight went off again, leaving me in darkness. I looked around for any sign of a light, but there was nothing. Just total blackness with only the stars overhead. Which way was the pickup? I was kind of disoriented, not sure which way I'd come from and which way I'd been running.

I stood still, not moving, holding the dark GPS in my hand. I was still breathing hard from all that running, and I couldn't make myself move. It was scary out here in the dark with no light to see by. I heard a clicking sound above me and I looked up. I couldn't see a thing.

But I was pretty sure I knew what that sound was. Bats. There were probably dozens of them up there above me, flying around and scooping up insects by the hundreds, giving off their little sonar waves so they didn't crash into rocks or trees. I wished I had sonar.

This was high desert, and it was dark. So dark I couldn't see my hand in front of my face. I couldn't even see the bats that I knew were flying right over my head.

All of a sudden, I was too scared to move. What if I came across a coyote? What if I stepped on a scorpion? Or a rattle-snake!

I stood frozen in place, unable to take a step forward or even turn the backlight on again. I started shivering, even though it wasn't really cold. I rocked back and forth a little, clutching my GPS.

I couldn't calm myself down. Two miles? I didn't want to hike two miles in the dark across desert terrain to get to the 60! Then what? I could maybe flag down a passing car, but what if it was a psycho killer who stopped to pick me up? I'd already escaped from one psycho tonight. I didn't have it in me to get away from some new one.

"I wish my dog was here," I said, and the sound of my small voice, whimpering and high-pitched, didn't comfort me at all. I was starting to feel lightheaded. Maybe I had brain damage from that blow to the head. I'm going to lose con-sciousness and die out here all alone!

I pushed the backlight button on the GPS and stared at the screen. "You have to do this. It's going to be okay. You can do this." My voice sounded more normal now.

Calm down. Get a grip. And start walking.

With the backlight on, I moved to the navigation page. It could be so much worse. I could be out here right now in total darkness without a GPS unit in my hands.

I could do this. I could follow the arrow that would lead me the two miles to the highway. Coyotes would hear me walking and keep their distance. Snakes wouldn't be lying out in the open at night. Scorpions—okay, scorpions *would* be out at night, but at least I was wearing shoes.

The navigation arrow pointed east. I started to walk.

Chapter 25

I'd only been walking about twenty minutes when I noticed the low battery warning. Keeping the backlight on was using up extra battery power. If only I had my backpack with me. I always kept a spare set of AAs with me for emergencies like this.

But then I remembered—I'd left the batteries in the geocache when I'd taken out the bandana and beads to give to Jack. It was weird, but that actually made me feel a little better, knowing that I wouldn't have had extra batteries even if I'd had my backpack.

I decided to turn the backlight off and just concentrate on walking straight ahead. I knew I was going in the direction of the highway. I could turn it on every so often to make sure I was still on course.

It was hard walking across this strange terrain in the dark, so I had to take it slow. The ground felt bumpy and uneven under my feet. Once something sharp brushed past my bare leg and I stopped dead still, afraid I was about to walk right into a cactus. I inched carefully around whatever it was until I didn't feel anything else in my way.

Now I was totally over my little panic attack and it was

embarrassing to even think that I'd almost had a breakdown back there. I could do this. Everything would be okay if I just kept calm and didn't panic. Losing control was dangerous. I couldn't afford to make any crazy mistakes right now. I tried to think about just getting through this. And then once this was all over, I'd have a great story to tell everyone.

Clods of dirt and rocks sometimes tripped me up, but I edged along, putting one foot in front of the other. My head still hurt, but now it was just a dull ache across my forehead that I was almost used to.

Then I heard it. The sound of a car motor. I turned around, and way off in the distance a pair of headlights was moving forward. The truck! Steven was coming for me!

Instinctively I ran not forward but sideways, feeling like I had to stay out of the beam of the headlights. Then I dropped to the ground in a crouch and looked back. The headlights were still moving straight forward, bouncing a little across the unpaved road. I was well out of their range. If I just stayed put, I'd be invisible here in the dark. Was it the white pickup? I couldn't tell for sure. It was too dark and the vehicle was too far away. All I could see in the blackness were two beams of light shining on the ground in front of them.

As I lay crouching in the dirt, I watched the vehicle move farther away from me. Now I could see red taillights getting smaller and smaller until they were out of sight.

If that was Steven and the boys, I wondered if there'd been trouble when he woke up and found me gone. What had Jack told him? How was Sam now? All my crazy fears about them tracking me down and holding me hostage again or shooting me disappeared, but I still worried about the boys and what would happen to them.

Suddenly I felt bad for lying to Jack, for promising him I'd come back. But I had to save myself, didn't I? And he'd pulled a gun on me. I knew it was because he was scared to death, but that didn't make it any less dangerous.

Once I got out of this mess, got to safety, I could get help for Jack and Sam too. When the police heard the whole story, they'd track Steven down in that white pickup. Would the boys be okay with Steven until I could get help? I needed to keep moving.

I stood up and looked around me. Nothing but black night as far as I could see. I looked up at the sky and the millions and millions of stars. I've always loved looking at the night sky out where there aren't any lights to mess up the view, but tonight looking at all those stars overhead made me feel like a tiny pinpoint in the universe. I didn't really like that feeling, so to take my mind off how small and insignificant I was, I turned on the backlight of the GPS to check my course. I still had 1.8 miles to go to the highway. At this rate, it would take me hours.

I started walking again, turning the backlight off after I was certain about my direction. The low battery was making me nervous. If my battery died, then what?

I had to focus on the positive. For one thing, it wasn't cold outside. Also, it was a good thing I'd only hurt my head. What if I'd broken a leg or something? And I had my GPS. And Steven had pulled off the highway just outside of a town, which was a really lucky thing. I thought about how desolate some of the stretches of the 60 were—miles and miles of nothing. Even if I had to walk all the way into town, I was still within four miles. It easily could have been twenty or thirty. Things could've been so much worse.

I walked along in the darkness trying to keep myself in a

straight line, going in the direction that I felt was taking me closer and closer to the 60. I kept the light off as much as possible now. I'd only check it occasionally to make sure I was still heading in the right direction. I was really starting to feel okay.

Until—suddenly—the bottom dropped out from under me.

My feet touched nothing but air. I was tumbling through space.

I landed on my side with a thud. It took me a couple of seconds to figure out that I'd actually fallen. I lay there in the exact same position I'd landed in till my brain finally kicked into gear.

It all happened so fast. There must have been a ditch or an embankment or something that I'd fallen down. Just like that, suddenly there was nothing but air under my feet and I'd fallen.

I sat up and—

It was gone! My hands were empty! The GPS—oh my God, where was the GPS? I patted the ground around me slowly at first, and then when I felt nothing but rocks and dirt and gravel, I moved my hands around in wider and wider circles.

Nothing! Where was it? *Where was it?*

I was on my knees, my arms stretched out to their full length, sweeping them along the invisible ground in front of me in a wide arc. It had to be here. It had to be. I leaned forward so that I could reach farther. Any second now I'd find it.

Now I was slowly crawling around on my knees. Little pebbles dug into my bare skin. I kept moving my hands over the area all around me. Maybe it was just out of my reach.

"Come on! This can't be happening!" I yelled. My hand brushed against something smooth and cool, but when I got my fingers around it I could tell it was just an empty bottle. I tossed it out of range and kept desperately patting the ground around me.

Nothing! It wasn't there! I stayed on my hands and knees, afraid to move too far from the spot where I'd fallen. I had to find it! It had to be here!

Being careful not to move too far from the spot where I landed, I crawled around on my hands and knees and felt around in the dark space. My eyes strained to see something in the blackness in front of me.

Maybe I spent ten minutes looking. Maybe it was ten hours.

At some point, I just snapped. "NOOOO!" I bellowed at the top of my lungs.

And then I burst into tears. I stayed there on my hands and knees and sobbed like a two-year-old. Loud, racking cries that shook my whole body. Tears streamed down my face and my nose ran so much I had to keep wiping the snot away with my sleeve.

I had not cried like that in a long time.

The whole time I sat there bawling my eyes out, there was a part of my brain that seemed detached from the rest of me, and it was wondering, *how did this happen?* How did everything take such a sudden turn?

How did I get here? How did I go from being in my own safe bedroom a few hours ago to being out here—all alone in the desert? *How?*

"Help! Somebody help me!" I screamed. "Help me! Help!" I screamed till my throat was raw. "HELP!"

There was nobody to hear me. Nobody to help me. Nobody out here in the dark night to come to my rescue.

Hide and Seek

I was all alone with nothing—no food, no water, no light. And now no GPS. I had nothing. Absolutely nothing.

I cried until I was all dried up, and then I lay there curled up on the ground, my chest having little spasms from all the crying I'd done. I closed my eyes and lay still. I could die out here tonight and I wouldn't even care anymore. Let the coyotes and vultures feast on the leftovers.

Chapter 26

It was still dark when I woke up. I knew I'd been asleep, but I had no idea for how long. I lay there, flat on my back, staring up into the blackness.

Only now the black looked more gray. Was it my imagination or was the black not so black any more? I stared into it. It really did seem lighter. Maybe I was going crazy. Maybe it was an optical illusion.

I sat up. No, it wasn't my imagination. I could actually make out a few things around me now. I looked in the direction of the horizon, and part of it definitely had a lighter color to it. I sat still and noticed the sound of a bird trilling off in the distance. Little by little, I watched my surroundings come into view.

I could make out some bluish-gray bushes nearby growing close to the ground. Sagebrush, I thought. About three feet away I could see the ground rise up steeply. That must have been where I stumbled. I stood up and stretched. My hand reached up to feel the bump on my head. It was still sore, but it didn't feel quite as swollen as it had last night.

My throat was completely parched, and I tried to work up a little spit so I could swallow. What I wouldn't give for an ice cold bottle of water right now. But at least I didn't feel so foggy and confused. I felt semi-rested from having slept for a little while.

Now that I could see in front of me, I scanned the dark, coppery-colored ground for my GPS. I saw something round just inches away from me. I reached out for it. It was a rock. In the growing light, I could see that it wasn't an ordinary rock. It had veins of some mineral running through it. I knew there were mines all over around here, and I wondered if this might actually be worth something. It looked really cool, like no rock I'd ever seen before. It was roundish—a bumpy, slightly misshapen ball, a little smaller than a golf ball. Its surface was kind of smooth with a few little cracks in it. It had a gray color to it, and the veins in it were an even darker gray. It felt nice and heavy in my hand.

Weird that it'd been lying right next to me and that I hadn't felt it last night. I'd obviously missed it in the dark. I was glad it was daylight now and I'd been able to see it. I slipped it into my pocket.

But I still hadn't found my GPS, so I kept scanning the ground in front of me. When my eyes finally fell on its blue plastic casing, my heart actually leapt with relief. It wasn't easy to find, even with some light to see by. And no wonder—it was a good ten feet away from me. There was no way I ever would've found it in the dark.

I ran over and picked it up, so happy to have it again. The screen was blank. I pushed the power button but nothing happened. I kept pushing it, and then I remembered.

When I dropped it last night, it was on and the batteries were running low. Of course they were completely dead now. I felt a slight panic rise inside me, but I kept it under control.

Minute by minute, it was getting lighter, and soon it would be daylight.

Watching the world around me come slowly into view was the greatest feeling. It was such an amazing relief just to be able to see. I slipped my dead GPS into the pocket of my cargo shorts, but not the one that had the rock in it. I didn't want the rock scratching up the screen.

I looked around. The terrain here was so different from the mountains. Lots of open space. Hardly any trees, except for some Palo Verde with their smooth green trunks and long, wispy leaves that weren't leaves at all really—just green twigs. And a few dark-trunked mesquite trees with pale, almost green-gray leaves. Bare ground with a few wisps of straw-colored grass here and there. Lots of prickly pear and cholla cactuses scattered all over.

Overhead the sky was now the color of a pearl, and I could tell there were no clouds. Once the sun came up, it would be a beautiful clear day with a bright blue sky. And it was going to be warm. I swallowed again to ease my dry throat. How long was it going to take me to walk to the highway?

Which way *was* the highway? I didn't have my GPS to guide me now, so how would I even know which way?

Then I remembered. Last night, the arrow had pointed east—a little less than two miles to the east, and I'd get to the highway. East was...that way! Where the light was brightening up the horizon! I looked over my shoulder at the dark gray sky behind me. Yep, that was west. If I kept heading east, I should eventually get to the 60.

My head wasn't hurting as much now, but my dry throat made me feel pretty miserable. I tried not to think about it. I slipped my hand into my pocket and felt the rock I'd picked up. It made me feel calm to hold onto it. I felt a sudden surge of relief. I'd figured out which way to go on my own, without the GPS. And I could see! Things were good.

I started walking. Now the sun was just above the horizon, and the palest blue was seeping across the whiteness of the sky.

As I walked, I stared straight ahead, trying to see anything that looked like a highway. I thought I saw it, and I felt a sudden rush as I walked along, but then it disappeared. How could there be a mirage this early in the morning? My eyes were playing tricks on me.

But then after a while I saw something else that looked like a highway. And this time, it didn't disappear from view. When I saw one solitary car move down it, about half a mile away from me or more, I had no doubt.

My mouth twitched into a little smile. So close! The highway was just a short way off in the distance. "I can make it," I said, but my voice came out as just a raspy whisper. It didn't matter, though. I almost felt like laughing out loud, I was so happy and relieved to be this close.

There are good things and bad things about being able to see so far ahead of you when you're out walking in a desert landscape. The good thing is, you can see where you're heading from a long way away. The bad thing is, you can see where you're heading from a long way away.

I walked and walked and walked and walked, and always the highway was lying there in front of me, off in the distance.

Keeping my eyes on the horizon was not a good idea, I decided. I tried looking down at the ground for long stretches and then looking up again to see if I was any farther along. Sometimes it didn't look or feel like I'd made any progress at all. I gritted my teeth in frustration and kept going.

It was a real mind game to force myself to keep walking

and not look up every few seconds. At one point I started to jog, but the rough, uneven ground under my feet jarred me too much, and my head started to pound in pain. Running was definitely not a good idea. My scratchy throat was a constant distraction. I was as dry as the desert terrain around me.

But as I kept walking on and on, I realized I was getting gradually closer. And then I could really see it. I started to pick up speed. I had to get to safety before the sun got too high in the sky. I didn't think the temperatures in Globe got quite as hot as in Phoenix because it was slightly higher in elevation, but it was still really warm down here in mid-September. I figured it was somewhere in the seventies right now at daybreak. That meant it would probably heat up to the nineties by midday.

I kept moving at the fastest pace I could manage that wouldn't make my head hurt. And the whole time I kept the highway in view. With each stride I could tell I was getting closer and closer. A big truck rumbled down the highway, and I wondered if the driver happened to glance out his window and if he saw me off in the distance.

Finally, the highway was right in front of me. Then the pavement was in plain view. And then I was right at the edge of it!

I stopped and looked up and down the paved surface. This was definitely a highway; four lanes of pavement lay in front of me. This *had* to be the 60 I'd seen on the map page last night. I stood there, grinning. I'd never in my life been so happy to feel pavement under my feet. Civilization! This would take me to safety.

But—how? What next? Should I wait for a passing car and try to flag it down? The thought of hitchhiking made me really uneasy. I had this sudden fear—what if the next vehicle

I saw was a white pickup with a camper on the back? Would it stop? Would Steven jump out and grab me again?

I shook myself. That was just fear taking over. I'd seen the pickup pass me last night, or at least I thought it was the pickup. Which meant they were long gone.

I decided I didn't want to wait here for some passing car. According to what my GPS had shown me last night, I was just on the edge of Globe. I hoped that was true. I started walking in the direction that I thought would take me into town, keeping to the edge of the road.

All along I'd tried so desperately to get to this highway, but now it made me nervous to have my back to oncoming traffic. What if a car passed by—should I wave them down? Would it be safe to accept a ride from a stranger? Yesterday morning, my parents would've told me never to do that, but a lot had happened in the past twenty-four hours. These were extreme circumstances. Maybe I could ask to use their cell phone.

But I hadn't seen even one car since I'd reached the road. As I walked, I kept scanning the horizon for any signs of life. It was Thursday morning, probably about 6 a.m. Had Mom and Rick been up all night? Were Kendra and Shea totally freaked out about me? Had Shea told them about how mysterious I'd been acting for the past week, going off for long bike rides? Not that any of that information would help them figure out where I was.

And where were Jack and Sam right now? What was happening to them? Had Steven finally given in and taken Sam to a doctor?

Way off in the distance, I saw a building. I was too far away to tell what it was, but I felt a sudden charge. At least it was a sign of something! I picked up my pace a little.

I lost sight of the building when the highway dipped down a little, but within a few hundred feet I could feel the road climbing slightly again. Once I was over the rise of a hill, I couldn't believe my eyes! I could see all kinds of buildings about half a mile in front of me. This had to be Globe.

I started to jog, and at this point I didn't care if it made my head throb or my dry throat ache. I could see what looked like a service station. As I got closer, I was able to make out the sign. Circle K. Perfect! I ran faster, my feet pounding against the hard, bare ground on the edge of the highway.

I crossed the highway to get to the road that led to the Circle K, and then I stumbled across the parking lot. A couple of cars were parked outside. I could see lights on in the windows. My head was pounding, and now that I'd finally found my way to safety, I suddenly felt exhausted. A man walked out of the door carrying a cup of coffee, and when he saw me approaching at a jog, he stopped and stared.

I ran right past him and through the door. The store was completely empty except for a gray-haired lady behind the counter. When she saw me she put one hand to her heart, a look of shock spreading across her face. *She thinks I'm going to rob her,* I thought crazily.

"Good Lord in heaven, child! What happened to you?" She came out from around the counter, her hand out to me.

Okay, she doesn't think I'm going to rob her. I opened my mouth and in a voice that sounded like a rusty hinge, I croaked, "Do you think I could use your phone?"

Chapter 27

D arlin', what *happened* to you?" she asked again. Her hand reached out toward my head and I realized she must be able to see the bump.

"I had an accident," I said vaguely. "Please can I use your phone?"

"Oh my Lord! Who else was in the car with you? Is anyone else hurt?" she asked. Now she was standing in front of me, hovering in a grandmotherly way. She was about my height, and her forehead was wrinkled with a look of worry. She held her hand out just above my forehead, but she didn't touch it.

"No, not a car accident. Nobody else is hurt. Just me. Can I please use your phone?" I asked again.

Without a word, she walked back around the corner and picked up a phone from behind the cash register. "Can I dial the number for you?"

I was about to rattle off my home number when a thought flashed through my brain. I was actually closer to Dad's house in Scottsdale now than to my own house in Greer. And I wanted someone to come get me right this instant. I gave her Dad's cell phone number instead. I'd call Mom and Rick as soon as I got off the phone with him.

She punched in the number and handed me the handset. It only rang once before Dad picked up. "Hello?" I heard my father's voice yell right in my ear.

"Dad? Hi, sorry to call so—"

"Chase? Chase, is that you? Where are you? Are you okay?"

"Yeah, Dad. Look, the reason I'm calling so early—"

"Where are you?" Dad was screaming at me. "What number are you calling from?" It was weird that he'd react this way to getting a phone call from me early in the morning.

"I'm at a gas station. I had a"—how could I even start to explain this?—"weird accident, and I'm at this Circle K." I held my hand over the receiver for a second. "Are we in Globe?" I asked the lady who was staring at me like I was a Martian invader. She nodded vigorously.

"I'm at a Circle K near Globe, Dad. Just off the 60. Do you think you could come get me?" My voice cracked a little, and I was afraid that any second I'd burst into tears again like I had last night, and here I'd be, bawling my eyes out in front of this nice, freaked-out lady with my dad listening on the other end of the line.

"Oh my God! Globe? What are you doing in Globe, Chase? Listen, your mom called me about an hour ago, told me you'd been missing *all night!* I'm in my car on my way to Greer right now!" Dad was talking a hundred miles an hour. I'd never heard him sound so frantic before.

"You're on your way to Greer? Can you call Mom and Rick? Tell them I'm okay?"

"Yeah, yeah, sure, but what's going on? How'd you get to *Globe*? Are you sure you're okay?"

"Yeah, I'm okay." I took a deep breath. "Dad, believe me. It's a long, long story. It's going to take me hours to tell it all. Please just come and get me."

"Okay. Absolutely. I'm on my way. Where are you? What's the address?"

I asked the nice lady for the address and repeated what she told me to Dad. I could tell he'd probably pulled over and was putting the address into the GPS he had in his Lexus. Thank God for GPS units! They made life so much easier.

"How long will it take you? Can you get here fast?" I asked him.

"It looks like I'm an hour and fifteen minutes from where you are. I'll get there as fast as I can."

I reminded him to call Mom and Rick as soon as he got off the phone with me, and then I hung up, but not before telling him about sixteen more times that I really was okay.

I handed the phone back to the lady. "My dad's coming to pick me up," I told her. "Do you think I could have a bottle of water?"

And then she was rushing around, getting me water and a cup of ice and some paper towels. "Honey, we should put something on that bump. It looks terrible!"

I was so glad to have someone like her working here. I doubted a man would've fussed over me like this.

I opened up the water bottle and drained half of it before I answered her. "Really? Is it that bad? It hurt a lot last night, but it feels better this morning."

"Go take a look in the restroom," she said, pointing me toward the men's room.

When I flicked the light switch, I couldn't believe what I saw in the mirror. Not only did I have a lump on my forehead, but my whole right eye under the lump was black and blue! No wonder she'd stared at me like that. And the guy with the coffee too. I really was a sight.

"Whoa," I said out loud, taking a closer look at it. I'd never had a black eye before. The whole socket was blackened and bruised. I had to admit, it looked pretty cool.

My face was dirt-streaked, my hair was sticking up all over, and my T-shirt was so grubby it looked like I'd been wearing it for a week. I really did look awful, and I'd only been gone about twelve hours. Good thing I hadn't spent a whole week lost in the desert; I'd scare small children.

I didn't want to freak out Dad when he got here, so I washed my hands and face in the sink and rubbed my damp hands through my hair, trying to smooth it down. But there was no way to hide my black eye.

When I came out of the restroom, the lady was waiting on a customer at the register. After the guy walked out, she looked at me with that same wrinkled forehead.

"Can I get you anything, sweetheart?"

I glanced at the bakery cabinet. "I'd love a doughnut. I don't have any money on me, but my father will pay for it when he gets here."

She bustled over and took the chocolate-covered donut I was pointing to out of the glass cabinet; then she even went to one of the coolers and got me a plastic bottle of milk. When she saw the way I scarfed that down, she warmed up a frozen burrito in the microwave and gave me that too. I was finally starting to feel a little more normal.

I leaned against the store's front counter on my elbows. For now I was glad that there weren't any customers coming into the store. I really wanted to sit down, but there wasn't any place for me to sit, so I just stood there and tried to make conversation with the lady.

Since I knew she was dying of curiosity, I decided I'd tell her a little bit about what happened. I didn't want to tell her the whole, involved story. I had a feeling I was going to have to tell it to a lot of people before the day was over.

"Well, that must've been some bump on the head. You better get yourself to a doctor as soon as you can and get it checked out. Blow to the head like that—it could be dangerous. Not something to mess with." She pursed her lips and shook her head knowingly.

She made me an ice pack out of a plastic bag and some crushed ice and insisted I hold it on my forehead, even though I doubted it would do much good now. She took me to a little room in the back for employees and I sat down in a chair there, propping my elbows on the table to hold the ice pack on my bump. She'd been so nice to me, the least I could do was humor her.

But I was starting to feel sleepy, so I put my head down on my arms and fell asleep right there even with all the fluorescent lights shining. I didn't wake up until I heard her calling, "Sweetheart, your father's here."

My dad came in right behind her and grabbed me, lifting me up out of the chair and hugging me tight so I could smell all his familiar smells—his starched dress shirt, his Polo cologne, and the Altoids he chewed by the handful.

"My God! What happened to you?" he yelled as soon as he got a look at my face.

"I got a bump on the head," I said, still holding onto him. I was so relieved to see him. Finally, I felt safe.

Chapter 28

My father paid the lady for all the food and drinks like I knew he would, but she kept telling him it wasn't necessary "after all the poor boy's been through," even though she didn't know the half of it. Finally, she gave in and took Dad's money, and as we were walking out, she said, "Now get that boy to a doctor and see about that knock on the head. You can't mess around with that."

Dad told her he would, and we went out and got in his car. The bright light of mid-morning made me squint. It was as warm as summer, just as I'd predicted.

Dad turned on the engine and cranked up the air conditioning. Then he picked up his cell phone and handed it to me. "Before we go anywhere—call your mom. I promised her I'd have you call the second I got to you."

So I did. Mom started crying when she heard my voice, and I felt so bad she'd had to worry about me. After we'd talked for a couple of minutes, I finally got up the nerve to ask her, "Mom...did Dexter make it home okay?"

From the way she paused, I knew the answer before she said anything. "We figured he was with you. But I'm sure..." Her voice trailed off and she didn't say anything else.

Hide and Seek

"Well, say hi to Rick and the girls for me. I'm okay. Really." My throat felt tight. I had to change the subject because I couldn't stand to think about what might have happened to Dexter.

As I listened to Mom's voice on the other end of the line saying, "Oh, thank God! Thank God! Are you really safe now?" I was suddenly hit by a weird sensation of déjà vu. Why was this so familiar? Why did it seem like I'd had this conversation before?

Then I remembered. My phone call to Jack and Sam's mom. It was so much like this call with my own mom. Had that just been yesterday afternoon?

Dad took the phone from me, and while he was telling Mom about my bump and the black eye, I thought about Jack and Sam's mom. Sure, she'd had good news yesterday, but her kids weren't home yet. She still hadn't talked to *them* on the phone. And they'd been gone months, not hours. I suddenly felt like I was going to cry. I cupped my chin in my hand and propped my elbow on the armrest, staring out the window and letting the bright sun blind me while the cold air from the dashboard vents blew in my face.

When Dad got off the phone, he said to me, "Okay. It took some convincing, but I got your mom to agree to let me take you back to Scottsdale and have a doctor there check you out inside of driving you all the way home first."

"Do I really need to go to a doctor? It's just a bump on the head."

"Yeah, you really do. Besides, Chase, I promised the lady at the Circle K." Dad broke out laughing and put the car in reverse, backing out of the parking space. Once we were heading toward the 60, he looked over at me.

"Son, start talking. I want to hear it all."

So I started at the beginning—the very beginning of that first day when I'd found the geocache and the half-written note asking for help. I told him about writing notes and finding more notes until I came across the two hungry kids who said they were camping.

"From the start, it just seemed weird," I told Dad. "The way they worried about snoops and didn't like cops. But I watched them at their campsite one day, and they *looked* normal. I had this theory that maybe they were just homeless."

I told him everything—about the shoplifting incident, about first seeing the flyer for the missing-children's website and looking for them and not finding anything. About changing license plates and "moving on."

"So Jack and Sam and I came up with a plan for me to look for them at a new campsite." I explained how we used the bandana, the beads, and the duck call. Then the hunch I'd had about the Packers. And seeing their picture on the website and making the phone call to their mom.

"When I was actually able to find them again, I was so happy and excited. Until I found out that Sam was sick. Then their dad showed up, and when he saw me—some stranger— he lost it. The next thing I knew, I was in the back of the truck."

"I still don't know what happened to Dexter," I said quietly. I could feel Dad glance at me, but I didn't look at him.

"I'm really worried about Sam, Dad. He was so sick. He kept throwing up, and he had a really high fever. His dad gave him some Tylenol, and he fell asleep, but he really needs to see a doctor. Think he'll figure that out and take him to one?"

Dad shook his head. "Who knows? This guy sounds like he was on the verge of a breakdown. Knocking you out! Taking you with him—was the guy out of his mind? Did he seem unstable?"

"Well, he seemed…like he didn't know what he was doing. At first he seemed like he felt bad for hurting me. But then when I told him Sam needed a doctor, he just lost it and started screaming at me. He said he hadn't slept in two days. I think Dexter and I caught him totally off guard. I get the feeling that if Dexter hadn't been barking at him like he was about to attack, the guy probably would've just chased us away and then left with his kids."

Then I told him about us stopping so Steven could sleep. But when I got to the part about Jack pointing the gun at my head and threatening to shoot me, I couldn't tell that part. I don't know why, but I couldn't. So I changed it a little.

"So anyway, as soon as his dad fell asleep, Jack…let me go, and I took off running. And since I had my GPS with me, I was able to figure out where I was. It was just like you said— I might need it in case I ever got lost in the boonies." I looked over at him, and he was gripping the steering wheel so tight it looked like his fists were glued to it.

"Amazing, Chase! I can't believe you went through all that. I'm forty-three years old, and I've never had an adventure like that! It's amazing! So you used the GPS and got yourself to that Circle K?"

"Well, it wasn't that easy. While I was walking last night— you know, it was pitch black and I didn't have a flashlight or anything except the GPS backlight to see by—I stumbled down a little hill. I dropped the GPS and couldn't find it in the dark. I fell asleep and when I woke up this morning, I found it, but the battery was dead. I knew I needed to go east, so I was able to follow the sun and get to the 60 and then walk the rest of the way to the Circle K."

"You spent the night all alone in the desert! Buddy, I can't believe how brave you were through all that! I'm so proud of you." He reached out and smacked me on the leg.

"I'm not brave," I said.

And then I couldn't hold it in any more. The tears came pouring out of me, and I cried as hard as I'd cried last night. I turned my face away from my father, but there was no way I could hide it. While I sat there sobbing, I could feel his hand on my shoulder, rubbing my neck, ruffling my hair, but I couldn't get hold of myself. I couldn't stop crying.

"It's okay. It's okay. I know you're exhausted. And hungry. And..." He was searching for the words to calm me down.

"No I'm not! I'm not any of those things. I'm just...." I could see my red, teary face in the side mirror, and I looked away. "I made so many stupid mistakes!"

Dad let out a surprised little laugh. "Stupid mistakes? Chase, don't be so hard on yourself. It sounds like you did everything right."

"No I didn't! At one point last night, I totally froze. I could hear bats flying overhead, and I started thinking about coyotes and rattlesnakes, and I was paralyzed! I almost had a breakdown right there. And then later when I dropped the GPS, I broke down and cried my eyes out, just like I'm doing now! I probably cried for an hour!" Now I was exaggerating a little to make it sound worse than it was. It'd probably been for more like ten or fifteen minutes, but the point was, it *felt* like an hour.

"Well, considering your circumstances, I think anyone would've reacted that way. I know I would've."

"No, you wouldn't. I lost it. I can't believe I broke down like that." My voice kept cracking, and I hated the sound of it.

"What happened after that?" Dad asked quietly. I was glad that his eyes were on the road ahead of him instead of looking at me. It was nice to be in the car, with both of us staring out the window. It made it easier to talk, not having to look at each other.

"I fell asleep. And when I woke up, it was morning."

I pulled the rock I'd found this morning out of my pocket and looked at it. The veins running through it were silvery. The rock had a nice heavy feel to it, and I tossed it back and forth from one hand to the other.

"And then after that, you were alright, weren't you? You figured out which way you needed to go, even without the GPS."

I shrugged and leaned my head against the window. "I guess so."

"Chase, don't you see what a great job you did? Okay, so you had a few minutes of panic and you broke down a little. You still managed to get out of a stretch of desert when you were all alone, and you had no idea where you were. *And* you had a head injury."

I could feel myself smiling a little. "Not a head injury. Just a bump."

"Well, that's a god-awful looking bump, let me tell ya," Dad said with a laugh. "I'm just…amazed. Amazed that you got through it all so well. I'm so proud of you."

I squirmed in the seat a little. I was embarrassed to hear him say that. But at the same time, hearing it did make me feel a whole lot better.

"And you should be proud of yourself. And not just because of the way you took care of yourself last night. Also the way you wanted to help those boys out. You felt a sense of responsibility toward them because they were a couple of young kids who needed some help. That was a really mature thing to do."

I could feel my face getting warm. I opened my palm and looked at my rock, examining its veins. I really did want to help Jack and Sam, but I hadn't done a very good job of that.

"Yeah, but I made lots of mistakes with them too. I guess I didn't really help them. I wanted to, but I did lots of things wrong."

"Like what?"

"Like I kept thinking I should tell Mom and Rick what was happening, but I didn't. I didn't really want to. I *liked* keeping it a secret. I acted like this was all some big game I was play-ing. I had all these crazy thoughts about how I'd sneak the kids into one of our cabins and keep them there for the whole winter, bringing them food and supplies they needed. Like they were some stray cats I'd found that I was taking care of. Don't you think that's stupid?"

Dad smiled at the stray cats expression. "No, it's…it shows your kind heart. And yeah, you should've told Mom and Rick what was up, but you still did a lot of things right."

"Really? It doesn't feel like I did one thing right," I said. I wanted to hear any nice comment he might think of to say to me now. I needed to hear it.

"One thing! How about twenty things? That thing with the bandana and the beads and the duck call? That was absolutely brilliant! How'd you even come up with that?"

I looked away so he couldn't see me smile. "Well, that was a pretty good idea. I guess."

"And figuring out Wisconsin from that one comment about the Packers? How'd you even remember that? And guiding yourself with the GPS. And figuring out you needed to go east by looking at the sun. Chase, don't you see? You were amazingly levelheaded through this whole ordeal."

I let out a long sigh. "Except the crying part." I tossed my rock from one hand to the other.

"Oh, don't give me that. You think real men can't cry?" He glanced over at me. "I cry lots of times when I say good-bye to you and your sisters."

"You do not!" I said, laughing a little at the thought. But he just stared straight ahead and didn't answer me. "Are you kidding me? Do you really?" Maybe he was being serious.

When he didn't say anything, I felt so sad all of a sudden. So sorry for him. It was always hard to say good-bye to Dad when we left him, but I hadn't cried in years. Not since I was a little boy. There were times when my chest felt tight and my throat would get all achy, but I was always okay with it.

"I never knew that, Dad," I said quietly.

"Well, it's hard to….," he started off. But then he got quiet and didn't say anything else.

We rode along in silence for a long time. I slipped my rock back into my pocket and positioned the air conditioning vents so the cool air was blasting right in my face. Then I rested my head against the back of the seat. I felt suddenly exhausted. But in a good way. I felt good about a lot of things.

Chapter 29

So much stuff happened in the next few days it was hard to keep track of it all. Dad took me to a doctor when we got to Scottsdale. He called the knot on my head "impressive," asked me a couple of hundred questions, and then told Dad he could take me home. "But get him straight to an emergency room if his vision gets blurry or if he starts talking out of his head."

We went back to Dad's condo and I took a really long nap. And then we made the long drive up to Greer. When we were in the car that afternoon, a man called Dad's cell phone and asked to speak to me. It was the detective from Wisconsin who'd been working on the "Makovec case," as he called it. He'd called Mom first, and she'd given him Dad's number to reach me.

I had to tell him my whole story. I told him how sick Ryan was and how I'd tried to convince Steven to take him to a doctor. He asked me all kinds of questions about the pickup.

"It was a Toyota," I blurted out suddenly. I'd remembered seeing the Toyota logo on the tailgate when I'd climbed out.

"Do you remember what kind of model it was? Like maybe a Tundra or a Tacoma?" he asked.

"Not really. But I might be able to pick it out if I saw some pictures of trucks," I told him. I described the cab, and he said it was regular, not extended, so that helped. I'd never really gotten a close-up look at the license plate, so I couldn't give him any letters or numbers of that. But I told him how Steven apparently switched out plates often, and that I was sure it had an Arizona plate on it now.

"Wow. This is a lot of help, Chase. These are some really good details to go on. You sound like a fine young man."

"Thanks," I said. It embarrassed me a little to hear it, but it made me feel pretty good too.

We got into Greer on Thursday evening. Coming home really was like having a hero's welcome. Mom, Rick, Kendra, and Shea ran outside to greet us when we pulled up the long gravel driveway. All four of them piled on me at once and smothered me with hugs and kisses.

"Your eye looks terrible!" Mom said through clenched teeth. She was holding my face between her hands and wincing as if it hurt her just to look at it.

"Let me see!" yelled Shea, trying to wiggle in between us.

"Eh, makes him look pretty tough," Rick said, trying not to smile when Mom gave him a look.

"The phone keeps ringing—you wouldn't believe all the calls," said Kendra. "Everybody at school has heard about it now. You're going to be a celebrity after all this."

It was great to see everyone and to finally be home. But someone was missing. I looked around for Dexter. He was nowhere in sight.

"Dexter didn't come home yet, did he?" I said, bracing myself for the bad news.

Rick looked at the ground and cleared his throat. "We

haven't seen any sign of him. Yet. He'll probably show up soon though."

"We need to go get my bike. We can look for him," I said, ready to jump back in the car, but a part of me had this horrible sinking feeling. Dexter could find his way home easily; he'd just have to follow his own scent trail. If he hadn't come back after being gone for twenty-four hours, I was afraid I knew the reason why.

"Honey, we can't go now. It's dark. We'll get your bike in the morning." Mom looked at Dad, who was leaning against his open car door. "Brian, you're not driving back to the Valley tonight are you? We've got plenty of room in the cabins."

Dad looked a little embarrassed. "Um, sure. That sounds nice."

Dad actually seemed to like the idea of sleeping in one of the cabins, even if there wasn't a wireless connection. He and Rick were okay with each other. It wasn't like they were good buddies or anything, but they could stand being together—at least for a short amount of time.

After dinner, a couple of sheriff's deputies showed up because Mom and Rick had reported me missing last night. My parents had called the sheriff's office after they found out I was okay, but the deputies needed to follow up on what had happened to me. So I told them my whole story and everyone got to hear all the details of everything that had happened.

When they'd left and Mom and Rick were finished asking me all of their questions, I went to bed early. Even though I'd taken a nap at Dad's, I was still worn out. It took me about ten seconds to fall asleep, but later I woke up to go to the bathroom and I was kind of surprised to see that it was only 10:17.

When I came out of the bathroom, I could hear voices downstairs. At first I thought it was just Mom and Rick, but then I heard Dad's voice too. I stopped at the top of the stairs and waited to see if I could hear anything they were talking about.

It sounded like Mom and Rick had been amateur detectives on their own. "So you talked to the kids' mom?" Dad was saying. "Last night? Did she call here?"

"No, we called her. When Chase didn't come home last night, we started calling his friends, and I saw on the caller ID that there was a number with a strange area code," Mom told him. "She said Chase had called her and talked to her that afternoon."

"So we thought there had to be a connection between him being gone and this woman with the missing kids," I heard Rick say. "I checked the history on the computer and saw that someone had been on this missing children's website. That's how we started piecing things together."

Then the three of them started talking about "charges." Kidnapping, assault with a deadly weapon. "Should we press charges if they ever catch this guy?" Mom asked.

"Absolutely!" I heard Dad's voice. "This guy sounds like a real nutcase."

"Well...," said Rick, like his mind wasn't made up yet.

I sat silently at the top of the stairs listening to it all. Wow. It was a good thing I hadn't told Dad about how Jack had held the rifle to my head.

I still couldn't really believe that part. How could he have turned on me like that? I was his friend. I'd always helped him. If Sam had been awake, would Jack have acted that way? Sam seemed to really like me and look up to me, more so than Jack. I couldn't imagine *him* threatening me with a rifle. But then he was just a little kid.

"Did Chase tell you anything else about how this guy

treated him?" asked Mom. She'd asked me all that at dinner, but I could tell from her voice that she wanted to hear every last detail that Dad might have gotten out of me.

"Not a lot. He said the guy seemed sorry at first that he'd hurt him, but then he got out of control about the sick kid."

That made me wonder about Sam. How was he now? Was Steven taking care of him? At least he'd tried to get him medicine, but would he get help for him once he realized how bad he was? After he got some sleep, would he finally be able to think straight?

They were still talking, but I crept down the hall to my room and climbed back into bed. It was a little weird knowing that all three of my parents were downstairs in the same room right now because that had never happened before. But it was also a good feeling too. Thinking about my family made my eyes sting with tears. I'd always known they loved me, but now I was really aware of it.

What about Steven? What kind of dad would do that to his kids? Was there some reason he wanted to take them away from their mom? I wondered what Jack and Sam's lives had been like before with their mom. I remembered what Jack had said—about how I could live with them now and Steven would teach me how to fish. He'd told me that Steven only yelled some of the time.

I had no idea what Steven was really like. Had he shot Dexter? What would he have done to me if I hadn't gotten away? Before all that happened, I'd made up this little story in my mind that he was this poor guy whose wife had died and who was possibly homeless, who was just trying to take care of his kids the best he could. But what was his real story? What had happened between him and the boys' mom that would make him run away with them?

Hide and Seek

The next day was Friday, and not only did I get to stay home from school, Mom even let Kendra and Shea have a day off too. She called the whole episode a family emergency and said the girls wouldn't be able to concentrate anyway.

That morning we went to pick up my bike. We drove out in the Durango to the forest service road, and my bike was right there, lying by the side of the dirt road where I'd left it. I glanced around cautiously, half-afraid I'd see my dog lying dead nearby. Then we walked the short ways to where the tent had been pitched, and we found my backpack.

I whistled and called for Dexter, but I had this feeling that he wasn't going to come running up. I could just sense that he wasn't around.

Dad left later that morning. Kendra, Shea, and I hugged him and said good-bye. "So we're on for the weekend in November I told you about?" Dad asked me.

"Sure! You got the tickets for the Lakers game, right?"

"Yeah, I did. And the Brophy Open House sounds okay for Sunday?" he asked.

I nodded. "It might be interesting to see the school." For days, I hadn't thought about Brophy or about moving. But I guess it was time for me to start.

"Keep me updated about any other developments," Dad told Mom.

"I will," she told him.

As we watched Dad pull out of our driveway, I wondered if he'd been telling me the truth about crying when he said good-bye to us, or if he'd made that up to make me feel better. In some ways, maybe it would be a good thing for all of us to move back to the Valley.

After Dad was gone, I gave Mom a big hug. "I'm glad you and Dad are friends," I murmured into her shoulder. She held me tight for a long time, and for once, Shea didn't butt in and insist on being hugged too. I'd never really thought that much about how Mom and Dad got along. Till recently.

As we were going inside, Rick stopped me and said he wanted to talk to me for a second. Mom and the girls went inside while we stood outside in the mid-morning sun. "You know you should've told your mom and me about those kids as soon as you thought something wasn't right. And you never should've taken off like that without telling us where you were going."

"I know. It's just—things really snowballed on me all of a sudden."

Rick nodded. "I understand that. And even though I wish you'd never gotten yourself into that situation in the first place, I'm still really proud of you. I'm so impressed with the way you handled yourself through all of this when things did get out of hand. You did a great job, Chase. Really. You should be proud of yourself."

"Thanks," I said. I didn't bother arguing with him about whether he should be proud of me or not. I was beginning to feel like maybe I had done a few things right.

When we went inside, I went up to my room to be alone for a while. My dead GPS was lying on the nightstand beside my bed, so I picked it up and looked at it. I'd have to remember to put new batteries in it before I used it again. But I wasn't sure when I'd be using it. It'd been great to have it, and it set me off in the right direction. But in the end I'd had to find my own way. Without any fancy gadgets. I'd just had to do it all on my own.

I took the rock I'd found out in the desert out of my pocket and examined it. I'd started carrying it around with me in my pocket. I wasn't sure why I liked the rock so much. It was just a rock. But it was cool looking. I liked its round shape and heavy weight. And also it reminded me of my night alone in the desert. It sort of felt like my good luck charm.

Thinking about that night in the desert made me think of Jack and Sam again. What was going on with them now? We had their mom's phone number, and we could find out from her what the latest news was. I was about to go downstairs and ask Mom about calling her when I heard a knock.

Mom opened the door, and she had a little smile on her face. "Chase, there's someone here who wants to see you."

I sat up just in time to see Dexter pushing past her through the open door.

"Dexter!" I shouted. He limped over to me, his tail wagging slightly. I jumped out of bed and hugged him, burying my face in his dusty, warm fur and breathing in his smelly dog scent. I'd never been so happy to see anyone in my life. He was alive! I'd been so afraid that I'd never see him again. I couldn't let go of him, but then I watched the way he held his front foot off the floor, careful not to put weight on it. "Mom, he's limping! He's hurt!"

"I know. He came limping up the driveway just a few minutes ago. No wonder it took him so long to get home."

I checked him over carefully, not letting on to Mom that I was looking for a bullet wound. Whatever was wrong with his foot, it wasn't from being shot. I could tell that much.

I started scratching his chest, and then he rolled over to let me rub his belly. While I rubbed his chest, I tried to get a look at the front paw he'd been favoring. "Mom, I see it. It's a fishhook, I think. I can see the little round eyelet. Get Rick!"

The thought of Dexter having a fishhook stuck in his paw made my stomach feel all weak. Dexter got suspicious and rolled over, crouching on all fours again.

When Rick came in and heard that Dexter had a hook stuck in his paw, he went back downstairs to get a pair of pliers. Shea peeked in my door. "Is he okay? We should go to the vet. Right now." Kendra stood behind her.

"Hold on. Let's just see if it's a real emergency," said Mom.

Rick came back with a pair of the pliers. "This isn't going to be easy. He's hurt, and he doesn't want us near that foot. I'll hold him down, and you and your mom see if you can look at his paw."

I got him to roll over again, and Rick kind of laid on top of him, which made Dexter really freak out and start to thrash around. But when he calmed down for a moment, I gently took hold of his paw and got a good look at it.

"The hook's not stuck in the pads. It looks like it's tangled up in the fur between the pads." As soon as I let go of his paw, he started struggling again. It was hard for even a grown man to hold him still, but I took the pliers from Rick and moved in carefully. I was able to grab the eyelet part of the hook. I tugged at it slowly. Dexter yelped, but the hook came free.

"Got it!" I held it up for everyone to see. Rick stepped back, letting Dexter up. Dexter let out a short angry bark, then started licking his paw.

After that, he was walking almost normally again. Having the hook stuck between his pads must've been really painful, but it didn't seem like it'd really injured him. All morning I kept petting him, so relieved to have him home again.

If that wasn't enough stuff for one weekend, we got a phone call Saturday night from Laura Patterson, Jack and Sam's mom. Mom took it, and the two of them talked for a really long time.

When Mom finally got off the phone, she announced, "Well, there's some good news," but the way she said it didn't make it seem like she was about to deliver good news at all. "The father and the boys were stopped at the Mexican border last night near Nogales."

"Really? They found them?" I said, jumping up from the living room couch where we'd all been watching a movie.

"Yes, the police had notified the border authorities to keep a lookout for a white pickup with a camper and Arizona plates," said Mom.

"Did they arrest the dad?" asked Kendra.

"I don't know. I'm assuming he's in custody, but she didn't really tell me much about him." Mom had a blank look on her face and her arms were wrapped around her, like she was warding off the cold.

"What's wrong? Is it Sam? Is he okay?" I asked. I didn't like her expression.

"The mother mentioned Ryan. That's the little one, right? Apparently he was really sick when the authorities stopped them. He had to be airlifted to a Tucson hospital."

"Airlifted? In a *helicopter?*" I screamed. I could feel Rick and the girls looking at me.

Mom nodded. "Yes. I guess he had appendicitis and his appendix had ruptured."

"But he's going to be okay. He's in a hospital now. He's got to be okay," I insisted.

Mom looked at me wide-eyed. "It's pretty serious, honey. He has peritonitis now. He should've been treated for it a lot earlier."

I sank down on the couch and didn't say anything.

"What's peritonitis?" asked Shea meekly.

Mom went over and squeezed in beside her on the loveseat. "Well, it's an infection people can get from appendicitis. It doesn't happen very often. Usually when people have an appendicitis attack, a doctor removes the appendix and everything's fine. But if they don't get operated on soon enough, the appendix can actually burst and spread infection all through the person's body."

"Yuck," said Shea, shivering a little.

"I knew he was really sick. I knew he needed a doctor on Wednesday! He was throwing up and feverish then. And screaming in pain! Why didn't his father take him to a doctor then?" I grabbed a throw pillow off the couch and pounded it with my fist.

"At least he's getting medical attention now. That's something," said Mom.

"He'll be okay, won't he? It's not like he could..." I couldn't even finish the sentence.

"Let's hope so, sweetie." Mom rubbed her forehead. "That poor woman! I can't imagine what she's been through. She's in Tucson now at least. She flew out early this morning."

"So she's with them now?" I asked.

Mom nodded.

My mind was racing. I imagined how terrified Jack—Tyler—must have been when the truck got stopped. And then his little brother was taken away in a helicopter. What had happened to Tyler after that? The authorities probably took him away from his dad. His greatest fear had come true.

But at least he was finally with his mom now. And I felt better that I'd been the one to break that good news to him. Even if he didn't believe me.

"What's going to happen to their dad?" I asked suddenly.

Mom shook her head. "I don't know."

"He'll go to jail, won't he? He kidnapped Chase!" said Kendra. "And he kidnapped his own kids!"

Hide and Seek

"How can you kidnap your own kids?" Shea wanted to know.

"Their dad took them away without telling their mom where they were. And they were gone for over a year," Mom explained.

"Wow, that's awful," said Shea, shaking her head. I could tell she was thinking about our family, and how something like that could never happen to us. But why did it have to happen to Jack and Sam?

"It's just...really bad stuff. A lot for a family to go through. Everybody suffers—parents and kids. It's horrible," said Mom.

Rick let out a long breath. "The guy never could've crossed the border anyway with a rifle in his truck. He would've been stopped for that even if the authorities hadn't been looking for him."

"True," Mom agreed. "But if he's never crossed the Mexican border he might not have known that."

Rick pointed the remote at the DVD player and stopped the movie. "I don't think anyone feels like watching the rest of this. I'm ready for bed."

But I couldn't fall sleep until well after midnight. I thought about Sam in the hospital so sick. Did Steven feel bad for not getting him treatment? Was he sitting in a jail cell someplace now? He'd probably have lots of time to think about what he did. I wondered how it was when Jack saw his mom again. What had it been like? Did she bring his teddy bear along, and did he even remember it?

They'd been through a lot, those two kids. But at least now they were safe. I tried to think about that as I drifted off to sleep.

Chapter 30

Monday I went back to school, and I sure got a lot of attention for my black eye, which was starting to look more purple now.

"Dude, it looks so cool," Chris told me, but who cared what Chris had to say about it.

On the bus ride home, Carly Hudson asked me three times if I was sure it didn't hurt anymore. She was sitting in the seat across from mine, and Joseph Hernandez was four rows in front of us. "You're so brave!" she said. "I'm so glad you're back. Everyone was so worried about you last week."

"Really? Everyone?" I asked.

"Yeah. Me especially."

"Cool. Thanks for worrying about me." That was the most I'd ever said to her all year.

For the rest of the week, we didn't hear any more about Jack and Sam—Tyler and Ryan, as I tried to think of them now. A couple of times early in the week, I asked Mom if we could call their mom's cell phone just to check on how they were, but she said she didn't want to bother them. If Laura Patterson wanted to keep us updated, it was her choice.

"It's out of our hands now, Chase. You did your part to

help them. Now we just need to let them start putting their family back together again."

But one bit of news did get back to us from the sheriff's deputies: when they searched the truck, they found the rifle, of course, but it didn't have any shells in it. And they didn't find any other ammunition in the truck, either.

That news made me feel a whole lot better. I still hadn't told anyone that part of the story because I didn't want them to realize just how dangerous the situation was that night. I wondered if Jack had known that the rifle wasn't loaded. I didn't really blame him for what he'd done. He was just as scared as I was.

Thinking about Steven's unloaded gun actually made me laugh at times. Maybe he hadn't had a chance to steal any shells lately. What a tough guy.

Mom spent a lot of time on the phone with Dad that week, and whenever I was out of the room, I tried to listen in on her and Rick's conversations. I knew they were discussing whether or not to press charges against Steven for what he did to me.

The way I saw it, the guy was in enough trouble already for taking the boys away from their mom, and then he might be charged with kidnapping me as well. Even after all the bad things he'd done, I still felt a little sorry for him. He didn't seem like he was truly evil, just a guy who had made lots of mistakes.

Then Friday, when the girls and I got home from school, Mom was waiting for me at the door with a couple of overnight bags. "How would you like to go to Tucson?" she asked.

"Tucson? Why? What's up?"

"Laura Patterson called. Ryan's getting released from the hospital soon, and they'll be flying back to Wisconsin after that. She wants to meet you, if that's okay. So I thought I could drive you down there. Rick will stay here with the girls."

"Sure. Great! So he's okay, then? Ryan?"

Mom nodded. "He's going to be okay. It sounds like he was a really sick little boy there for a while, but he's gotten through the worst of it. Are you ready to go?"

So just like that, we tossed the bags in the car and took off. Mom said we'd stop in Scottsdale and I could spend the night at Dad's place tonight, and she'd stay with an old friend she used to work with. Then we'd leave for Tucson on Saturday morning.

It was a long car ride, and Mom and I talked about a lot of different things. The first subject that came up was Brophy.

"I know your dad loves the idea, but are you even interested in going to Brophy?"

I slumped down in the seat a little. "I don't know. I guess I'm curious about it. It wouldn't hurt to go to the Open House and see what it's like."

Mom nodded. "I don't know a lot about the school. I do know their academic standards are very high. They'd really get you ready for college if you went there."

"That's what Dad says. If I don't like it, do I have to go?" I asked, giving her a quick look.

"Well, we're not going to force you," said Mom with a little smile.

"One thing I'm not sure about," I told her. "How am I going to know if I'll like it or not unless I go there? And what if I go there and I hate it?"

"I suppose if you *hate* it, you'll tell us that and we'll take you out of there."

I leaned against the window. "It's kind of a big decision. If I do end up going to Brophy, will that mean we'll all move to Phoenix?"

"Well, it would be really hard for me to be so far away from you for four years. Rick and the girls would miss you too."

"Yeah, but Dad's away from all three of us now. And it's been like that ever since we moved up to Greer," I reminded her.

Mom sighed. "I know. That's definitely one advantage of us moving back to Phoenix. We'd all be close together."

"So—have you and Rick decided what's going to happen?" I asked cautiously.

"Honey, I don't know. If we can't sell, then we'll be staying where we are. At least for a while. But financially I think moving would be the best thing for the family in some ways."

I groaned. "I'm not crazy about moving. I'm going to miss Greer."

"Well, nothing's definite yet. We have to find a buyer first," said Mom, and I could tell how concerned she was about that. I felt a little guilty complaining about moving. If we couldn't afford to keep the store and the cabins any more, maybe we didn't have a choice.

When we got to Dad's that evening, Mom dropped me off and left for her friend's house. Dad and I didn't talk about Brophy at all. I guess he figured he wouldn't pressure me any more until the Open House. But I couldn't help thinking about all the changes that could be coming my way in the next year. I'd been trying not to think about these things, but not thinking about them wasn't going to keep them from happening. I might as well face up to it and figure out how I felt about it all.

Saturday morning, Mom picked me up and we drove to

Tucson to see Tyler and Ryan and to meet their mom. I was nervous about seeing those guys again—especially in a hospital room with a lot of strange smells and instruments around. Plus the fact that our moms were going to be right there with us.

I didn't know how Tyler would react to seeing me again. And I worried about how sick Ryan might still be. I hoped he wouldn't have tubes or needles or stuff coming out of him.

When we got to the hospital, I kind of stalled for a second. "We should've brought something—flowers or balloons. Aren't you supposed to take people flowers when they're in the hospital?"

Mom smiled. "Yes, but I doubt a little boy would be too impressed with flowers. Let's stop in the gift shop and see if we can find anything."

I kicked myself for not thinking to bring the tackle box full of the toys I'd given them. They might've liked to have that to keep. So when I saw a packet of green army men, I knew that had to be one choice. I also picked out a large plastic triceratops and some coloring books, puzzle books, and Mad Libs. "Something for them to do on the plane when they go home," I told Mom.

She nodded. "Good choice."

Then we went up to the floor where Ryan's room was. I was feeling jittery as we got close to the room. Mom knocked at the slightly open door, and a lady's voice said, "Come in."

We walked in, and there was Ryan propped up in bed, with Tyler and his mom in chairs beside him. I recognized her right away, since I'd seen her pictures on the website.

"Hi, Chase!" Ryan called from his bed, sitting up a little and grinning at me. Tyler smiled slightly.

"Hey, guys! Good to see you," I said, feeling really uncomfortable and unnatural. I wished I'd worn my Suns cap so I'd look like my old self, but I'd forgotten that too.

"Ooh, what happened to your eye?" asked Ryan. By now my eye was a kind of greenish yellow. It didn't look nearly as bad as it did last week, but it was still noticeable.

I glanced at Tyler, but he didn't say anything. "I got a bump on the head. It's better now, though."

Mom introduced herself to Laura Patterson, who came right over to me and grabbed me by the shoulders. "So, you're Chase. I am so happy to meet you." Then she hugged me, which made me feel pretty awkward.

"Nice to meet you," I mumbled.

"I brought you something," I said, handing Ryan the gift bag stuffed with the presents we'd picked out for him. "And these are for you," I said to Tyler, handing him the Mad Libs and puzzle books. "Something to do on the plane."

Ryan dug right into the gift bag and pulled out all his loot. "Cool! Army men! I love these guys!"

Same old...Ryan. I realized I'd probably always think of him as Sam. He had an IV needle taped to his arm and a plastic tube running out of it, but other than that, he looked pretty normal.

"Hey, you got a haircut," I said to Tyler. It was a stupid thing to say, but it was one of the first things I'd noticed about him—how clean he was, and how neat his hair looked. Ryan's was still shaggy like it had always been. I figured cutting his hair hadn't been a big priority this week.

Tyler smiled a little and rubbed his hand through his hair. I noticed a small white scar right below his hairline.

The two moms stood there watching for a few minutes, but

then they started their own conversation and moved to the other side of the room.

I looked at my two little buddies. Tyler had on all new clothes. They both looked different, all clean and everything. But still pretty much the same.

"So...how's it going?" I asked stupidly.

Tyler's one shoulder hitched up a little. "Pretty good."

So much had happened to all three of us since we'd seen each other the last time. I'd really been through a lot, but not nearly as much as they had. Plus I was older, better able to handle it all. It was amazing they were acting as normal as they were.

"You guys doing okay?" I asked. It felt like there was nothing we could talk about.

"Uh-huh," Tyler nodded.

"Hey, Chase—guess what? I've been real sick. I flew in a helicopter."

"Oh yeah? I heard about that. What was that like?"

"I don't remember. I was unconscience when it happened," said Ryan.

He meant unconscious. I eased myself down on the end of his bed. "How're you feeling now?"

Ryan sighed deeply. "Better. They took my appendix out. They've been giving me medicine through this thingy." He reached over and jiggled the IV tube a little.

"Be careful, Rye," said Tyler. "Don't pull it loose or anything."

So he'd gone back to calling him by his real name. Well, that made sense. But I wondered if it was as strange for them as it was for me.

I glanced around the room and took in all the balloons and stuffed animals all over the place. Then I noticed a dingy-looking bear with a green scarf around its neck and red mittens on its paws. "Hey, is that your teddy bear? The one you always slept with?" I asked Tyler. The bear might've been white at one point, but now it was a soft grayish color.

He nodded and didn't say anything.

"That's Fluppy," said Ryan. "And there's my raccoon. His name's Rascal." He pointed to the stuffed raccoon in the chair his mom had been sitting in. "Those are our old stuffed animals from when we lived in Madison. But look—we got some new ones now."

I smiled and leaned over to pick up the raccoon. "Rascal the Raccoon, huh? That's pretty cool. You can never have too many stuffed animals."

Tyler nodded in agreement but kept quiet. I wondered if he would say anything to me like, "Gee, sorry I pulled a gun on you," or "I didn't really mean it when I threatened to kill you," but he didn't. A normal person probably would've said that, but then he was just a little kid. I guess I could forgive him.

"Yeah, and you know what else? Tyler's birthday is tomorrow! And we're going to have cake and ice cream. And when we get home to Madison, he's gonna have a party at Peter Piper Pizza!" Ryan seemed more excited than Tyler.

Tyler looked embarrassed by all this information. I remembered seeing his birth date on the missing-children poster.

"Really? Happy birthday." I wished I'd bought him something better than just the puzzle books and Mad Libs. "My birthday's in September too. September sixth. How old are you going to be?"

"Ten," said Tyler, licking his lips a little like they were chapped.

"Cool. Double digits. You're getting pretty old, huh?"

Tyler nodded.

Wow, all that he'd been through in his life, and he wasn't even ten yet. But Ryan was even younger, only seven. I just hoped they'd be able to have a normal life now.

The moms came back to our side of the room. "We should probably be leaving soon," said Mom. "We have a long drive ahead of us."

"Don't leave yet," said Ryan. "You just got here."

"Thanks for the books," Tyler piped up suddenly. "I like doing these word search things. And connect the dots. I used to do those a long time ago."

We all looked at him. It was the most he'd said since I'd walked in. "You bet. Glad you like them. Hope you get a lot of cool stuff for your birthday."

His mom laughed. "Oh, don't worry. He will."

I stuck my hands in my pockets and felt something heavy—my rock. I pulled it out and without even thinking about it, I gave it to Tyler.

"Here, I found this in the desert. It's pretty cool—see the veins in it?"

Tyler turned it over and examined it, holding it up to the light so he could see it better. "Wow. That is cool. It's really heavy." He tossed it back and forth between his hands just like I'd done.

"It's my good luck charm. You can have it. It's not much of a birthday present, but...."

His mom laughed. "I thought only Charlie Brown got rocks on special occasions."

"Don't laugh! I like it a lot." Tyler looked up at me. "Can it be my good luck charm now?"

"Sure. It already brought me good luck," I said.

"Hey, I want a good luck charm too!" yelled Ryan from his bed.

"Sorry, buddy. It's Tyler's birthday. When it's your birthday, I'll…mail a rock to you."

Everyone broke out laughing over that, even Ryan. Tyler gazed at his rock, and I could tell he thought it was a good gift, not something stupid.

"Well, I hate to break up the party, but we really ought to get going," said Mom.

I felt that sudden achy feeling in my throat now that it was time to say good-bye. And I realized there was a really good chance I'd never see them again. "High fives, guys," I said, holding my hand out for each of them to slap.

Then I took Tyler's hand and shook it. "Since you're almost in double digits, we should shake. Like men." He grinned at me and ducked his head. I wanted to make sure there were no hard feelings between us.

As we were walking out, their mom followed us and grabbed me by the shoulders again. "Chase, I just want to thank you. How can I ever let you know how grateful I am that you called? And you saved Ryan's life!"

"No, I— "

"Yes, you did! You're the one who called to tell me about the first sighting of my boys. You let us know they were in Arizona and what kind of car they were in. If Border Patrol hadn't found him and gotten him to this hospital, he might have…" I could see she was about to start crying. She paused for a long minute and then took a deep breath. "I might have lost him forever. Thank you so much."

"You're welcome," I said, hoping I wasn't blushing.

"You saved his life. You really did."

I just stared at her, and then she hugged me and even gave me a little kiss on the cheek. When she let me go, I was too surprised to say anything else.

Mom wished her good luck and told her to have a safe trip back home, and then we left.

Walking out of the hospital, I could still feel the little wet spot on my cheek where she'd kissed me. I wanted to rub it off but I thought Mom might laugh at me, so I just let it air dry instead.

I'd never once thought over the past week that I'd been the one who saved Ryan's life. Maybe I'd helped, but so had a lot of people. The border authorities who stopped the truck, the airlift people, all the doctors and nurses who'd been taking care of him all week. It'd been a team effort. But I did feel good that I'd been part of the team.

When we got in the car and started the long drive back, Mom and I didn't say anything for a long time. Finally I broke the silence.

"I'm really happy for them, but it's sad too, you know?" I fiddled with the air conditioner vents because I was feeling really sad about saying good-bye to those guys.

"What is?"

"Well, it's great that they're going back to their home in Wisconsin and to their old life and everything, but…what's going to happen to their father?"

Mom shook her head. "Honey, I honestly don't know."

"Yeah, it was terrible what he did to them, taking them away from their mom and everything. And he sure didn't treat me too well either. But he's still their father." I leaned back against the headrest and stared out the window. "A guy really needs a father."

Mom sighed. "That family's been through a lot. If their dad can't be a good father to them, maybe someone else can step in—like an uncle or someone."

"I'm glad I've got Dad and Rick." I glanced over at Mom. "And you, too, of course."

Mom smiled when I said that. "You are fortunate to have three parents looking out for you. We'll always be here for you."

"I know you will," I told her. I thought about all the changes that might be coming my way soon. I was definitely going to need their help with all of that. But I also knew that from now on I could handle a lot more on my own.

Chapter 31

I climbed over the gray boulders looking for the right spot. The metal tackle box banged against my leg as I scrambled up the largest boulder looming in front of me. The rocks were smooth and rounded which made my feet slip a little, but pretty soon I was at the top of the highest boulder. Now from my vantage point, I looked down into the crevice below, formed where three of the gigantic rocks came together.

"Good hiding spot."

As soon as the words were out of my mouth, the wind snatched them and blew them off across the meadow. It was colder today than it had been. Strong winds were whistling through the yellow aspens and chasing the high clouds across the sky. At the sound of my voice, Dexter looked up and his ears perked a little, but then he went back to sniffing around at the layer of dry needles under a ponderosa pine.

I was about to lower the box into the crevice when I stopped myself and took one last look. Inside were two miniature Tonka trucks, two glow-in-the dark bouncy balls, some plastic dinosaurs, and two *Star Wars* action figures. There had been four at one time, but the rebel fighter pilot and the battle droid were gone now.

Hide and Seek

I'd put a couple of new items inside the box. A pen and a little memo pad full of blank pages. I snapped the clasps shut and lowered the box into the crevice. Next time I came back, the contents might be different. As people found my geocache, they'd take a toy and leave something else.

I moved the smaller rocks over the top to cover up the tackle box so that it was completely hidden. The first geocache of my own. I smiled a little, but I felt—not exactly sad. Just… it was hard to say. I looked around at the empty meadow and watched the dry grass bending in the breeze. Dexter stood by waiting for me, his tailing wagging and his mouth hanging open.

"Now we've got to mark the waypoint," I told him. I climbed across the boulders and jumped down. Then I walked several feet away into a nearby grove of trees before taking the GPS out of my pocket and marking the spot. It wouldn't be a challenge if I made it too easy to find. The waypoint should be near the geocache, but not right on top of it.

I picked up my bike and climbed on, and when Dexter saw that he dashed ahead of me. As my tires bounced across the bumpy ground, I looked back over my shoulder at the boulders behind me. It was a good spot. We'd be back some time to check on it; I just wasn't exactly sure when.

Now the only thing left to do was to go back home and log onto the geocaching website where I could record this new location so that other geocachers could find it. For the past couple of days, I'd been wondering about what to name it. There were two sets of names, after all, so I wasn't really sure which one to use. But as we moved across the field toward the hiking trail, I made up my mind.

"I know their real names are Tyler and Ryan," I told Dexter, as he ran beside me with his tongue hanging out. "But I've decided what I want to call it. 'Jack and Sam's Toy Box.'" Dexter looked up at me and panted. He seemed to understand exactly what I was talking about.

"To me, they'll always be Jack and Sam. "

More about Geocaching

Hidden treasure is everywhere. At present, there are more than a million active geocaches around the world. They can be hidden deep in forests, near busy city streets, on mountaintops, or even underwater—usually in places a traveler might otherwise miss. Some geocachers prefer sites with a little something extra, like a view of the ocean, an interesting rock formation, a beautiful waterfall, or a place of historical significance or cultural interest.

Geocaching is played by three to four million people worldwide. Anyone with a GPS can participate. Simply find the location of a geocache online, enter the waypoints into your GPS, and go. For longer hikes, be sure to take along a map, a compass, and some water. Take a friend along, or let someone know where you're going. Safety first!

Once you've found a geocache, you can log your find, take pictures, or trade items. If you take something from a geocache, be sure to replace it with something of equal or greater value and return the container to its original location.

It's important to respect the environment when you're geocaching. Be thoughtful about the surrounding area when you're looking for or hiding a geocache.

For more information, along with a searchable database of geocaches, look online at *www.geocaching.com.*

Happy hunting!

KATY GRANT is the author of the popular SUMMER CAMP SECRETS series for middle readers. She teaches college classes in composition and creative writing. She lives with her family in Arizona and enjoys visiting the White Mountains. *www.katygrant.com*